Honeycomb

A Collection of Short Stories

Linda Kelly

authorHOUSE

AuthorHouse™
1663 Liberty Drive
Bloomington, IN 47403
www.authorhouse.com
Phone: 833-262-8899

Published by AuthorHouse   09/29/2021

ISBN: 978-1-6655-3961-6 (sc)
ISBN: 978-1-6655-3965-4 (e)

Library of Congress Control Number: 2021920004

Print information available on the last page.

This book is printed on acid-free paper.

I dedicate this collection of stories to my sons,
Charlie and Alex and my husband,
Tim Kelly because they believed in me!

Contents

The Eerie Tales

The Mysteries of Ginny B.

Honeycomb

Honeycomb

—•—

*J*ay and Elise hiked through acres of cornfields, a shortcut to Warbler Woods, a nature preserve in the foothills of the Ozarks. Mr. Henry, their Biology teacher, had given their class at Lewis & Clark High School a field assignment. Their report on honey bees would be worth half of their final grade.

They were Team number 8 out of 14 teams in their class. They and the other teams would spend the entire day taking photos, videos and cataloging samples of flowering plants in their designated area. The purpose of the experiment was to compare their findings with those of two previous years to evaluate the effect of dwindling honeybee populations on the reproduction of wildflowers in forests habitats of Missouri.

Jay glanced back at the acres of cornfields he and Elise had just traversed. He pointed his cell phone and took a photo, grinned over at Elise and exclaimed, "That's one, only 999 more to go!"

Elise shook her head, "Sorry Jay." She wiped a trickle of sweat from her face, pulled back her long auburn hair into a ponytail and explained, "Cultivated crops don't count, and besides there are no flowers on these cornstalks."

At the end of the cornfield they hopped a chain linked fence which displayed a sign which read, "Warbler Woods Nature Preserve" and entered the park.

As they scanned the preserve, they saw an abundance of magnificent wild flowers, shrubs, trees and other flora.

"This is going to take hours and hours," Jay said. He took a sip

1

from his water bottle and continued with, "Remind me again what the point of all this hard work is."

Elise looked over at him, vexed that he hadn't reviewed the lesson plan and replied, "The point is to document how the loss of honeybees has impacted the amount of flourishing plants in this section of the forest." She pointed to a long wooden stake with a painted red tip that was posted in the ground about three feet away from them, "Here are the stakes that mark off our study area."

"I see them now," Jay zoomed in on the area with his cell phone, "They mark an area in the shape of a rectangle and extend into the woods." He jotted down the information in his notes and asked, "How can we tell if the number of flowers growing here has changed?"

Elise stood next to him and showed him the graph in her science notes, "We have data from 2 previous years to compare with our new findings." She paused, took a picture of a delicate Bluebell blossom and jotted down the date, time and the absence of any bees present on her log sheet.

Jay nodded, "Basically we count the flowering plants in the marked off area and later make a graph of this year's growth."

Elise pointed to the area, "You count this half to the 50th stake and I'll count the other half starting at that honeysuckle bush and finish on the right of that red maple." She started to walk to her marker but turned around, "I forgot to remind you to take a photo of each different wildflower. Those are our visual samples. We should get a good idea of the bee population from those too."

Jay shot a photo of a Black-Eyed Susan and commented, "And this is important to my life because…?"

Elise put her cell phone down with a frown, "Other than the fact that this report is 50% of our final grade? It's crucial to the future to document the ability of plants to thrive in our environment"

Jay waved his hand across the area and commented, "Maybe I'm just dumber than a box of rocks, but look around. There are hundreds of flowers around us. There should be plenty of bees in these woods, right?"

Elise scanned the area, "You do have a point there. You are not dumb by the way. You got an A on the Midterm, remember?" She sat down on a fallen tree branch and looked up at him.

Jay sat down beside Elise and asked, "Thanks, but explain to me again why bees are so important."

Elise checked her notes and reviewed, "It says in Chapter 12 that the population of honeybees has decreased 20% in the last 3 years, which could be catastrophic for farmers. They rely on bees to pollinate their crops, just like these wildflowers rely on bees to fertilize their blossoms. Bees fertilize all the fruits and vegetable we eat and all the edible crops and herbs we consume by the millions every year."

Jay looked over at her, "Without enough bees there would be less food to eat."

Elise took a sip from her water bottle and added, "Not to mention the medicines that are made from flowering plants."

Jay gave her a questioning look, "If there are fewer bees around, how do farmers get their crops fertilized so they can make food?"

Elise took a photo of a tiny yellow wild strawberry blossom and explained, "Farmers pay beekeepers, like my Uncle Johnny, to transport bee hives to their farms so they can pollinate their crops, she explained. "Fewer bees mean fewer crops and higher prices at the grocery stores. My uncle has had to charge a lot more for his services in the last 3 years. The higher price can cause small farmers to go out of business and lose their family farms."

Jay took a photo of a Beard-Tongue bloom and stated, "No wonder my mom is always complaining about how much fresh fruits and vegetables cost at the grocery store. We planted our own vegetable garden last year. Now she wants dad to plant a small grove of apple and pear trees on my grandma's seven acres in St. James."

"Now you are getting the whole picture," Elise grinned at Jay as they walked further into the woods. "Imagine how hard it is for poor people to feed their kids when prices go up."

Jay looked puzzled, "Okay, I get you, but why did the bees disappear in the first place?" Jay took a photo of an Ox-Eyed daisy and turned to her.

Elise laughed lightly, "Do you ever read the material in our textbook or the science journals?"

"Not during football season," Jay responded in surprise. "That's why I joined your study group!"

Elise grinned, "I thought it was because Ted and Ralph told you I was hot."

Jay laughed and replied, "Well, when I first saw you wearing those crazy goggles in lab and you weren't embarrassed, I figured you were cute and brainy."

"Flattery will get you nowhere, Jay Roberts." Elise kissed his cheek, and added, "When I saw you got that "A," I knew you were not just a mindless jock."

"So why did the bees disappear?" Jay asked.

"Scientists aren't really sure," Elise replied, "They call it Colony Collapse Disorder. Beekeepers woke up one morning and discovered whole colonies of bees had abandoned their hives leaving thousands of eggs and growing larvae behind. That is a crazy thing for bees to do." She paused a moment to take a picture of a delicately bloomed purple Spiderwort and continued, "Some botanists believe that overuse of insecticides, especially ones containing nicotine, created a toxic environment and the bees migrated. The nicotine doesn't harm animals so they thought it was safe."

Jay pretended to smoke a cigarette and said, "Nicotine? I guess the bees are non-smokers!"

Elise shook her head and said, "Very funny but this is serious." She took a gentle swipe at his arm and continued, "If all the bees disappeared or died, the food supply of our whole nation would be in real danger."

Jay finished taking notes on what Elise had explained, and asked, "If scientists are so smart, why can't they invent a machine that can pollinate the crops?

"They have," Elise returned, "Large agricultural firms use wind machines but it's costly and not as efficient as nature. Wasps, butterflies, and even woodland animals can spread pollen too, but not as well. It has to do with the balance of nature."

Jay looked over at Elise with a wry grin, "Now you sound like a narrator on the Discovery Channel! I get it. People messed up another thing that worked fine until we came along and screwed it up!"

Elise held up her cell phone, "Waves from cell phones could be another cause. All the output from cable, electrical wires and satellites bombard bee habitats. Bees are very sensitive to sound and vibrations."

"How can you tell?" Jay asked.

Elise answered, "I saw this fantastic video on Planet Earth. It showed you that bees have a special dance they do to talk to each other. If something interferes with that, the whole colony is hurt." Elise stood up and did a wiggle dance.

Jay got up and danced with her shaking his right leg, saying, "They do the Hokey Pokey too?" When Elise laughed, he suggested, "Maybe they all just got sick." He took a photo of a Trumpet Creeper climbing up a fir tree and added the data to this notes.

Elise nodded in agreement, "The entomologists, scientists who study insects, think that could be part of the problem, Diseases, parasites, insecticides and electronics combined could have overstressed the colony habitats."

"The bees have to be somewhere, right?" Jay asked. He looked closely at the patches of flowers. "Come to think of it, I haven't seen one bee yet, have you?" Jay checked his photos again to be sure.

Elise scanned and zoomed in on her photos and answered with a worried frown, "I don't see one bee in my photos either. We should have seen a few."

They both catalogued that information in their notes. Elise stood still and carefully scanned the area. She put her index finger to her lips and whispered, "Listen." She stood still and used the zoom lens on her phone to scan the area even those outside of their project area. She looked over at Jay, "No buzzing sounds! Not one bee in sight. This is really strange."

Jay looked at the ground, "Did the scientists find any dead bees lying around? I don't see any around here."

Elise checked her notes, and answered, "No. My notes say they disappeared without a trace."

Jay and Elise hiked the designated area for the next two hours. They documented and photographed myriads of wildflowers. They ventured deeper into the foliage, documented samples and took notes until the forest canopy grew so dense that only shade friendly plants grew there.

When they spotted a sunlit clearing with a bubbling brook meandering past the woods, Elise announced, "This is a great place to take a break and have lunch. It's already after one."

Jay and Elise found a fallen tree trunk nearby, and sat down to eat lunch. They munched on peanut butter and jelly sandwiches and talked about the upcoming Homecoming Game and Dance at their school.

Elise looked over at Jay, "Have you asked anyone to the dance yet?"

Jay shook his head, took Elise's hand and asked, "I know we're just friends, but will you go with me?"

"Sure," Elise squeezed his hand. "What are friends for?"

"Great!" Jay smiled and said, "Is this, like, a date?"

Elise laughed lightly, "Jay, if we go to the Homecoming Dance together we will be seen by the whole school! Not only are we officially dating but will be seen as a couple. Are you ok with that?"

Jay kissed her and murmured, "Cool."

Elise stood up and grabbed her supplies, "Come on boyfriend. Let's get back to work."

It was nearly 4 pm when they located another clearing and sat down for a break. They reviewed the photos, saved them to the project file and reviewed all the notes they had taken for their report.

Elise looked at a serene meadow that spread out before them. The tall buff colored grasses swayed in the afternoon breeze. Fall was bursting forth in the Ozarks. Magnificent colors were taking over the trees; crimson, orange, bright yellow, magenta and deep russet. Flowers bloomed in bright splashes of colors but there were no sight or sound of busy bees. Flies and mosquitos zipped by them and were gently batted away, and cicadas could be heard in the treetops, but no bees raced back and forth to the pollen filled blooms.

After the break, they walked along in companionable silence listening to cicadas, birds, frogs and the rustling of the leaves.

Jay noticed a section of bare ground up ahead and paused to look at it. He turned to Elise and waved her over, "This spot of ground over here is weird." The soil was grainy and looked turned over, as if a giant ant hill had been trampled and flattened.

As he moved the dirt around with his feet, Elise took a video of the strange flattened area. Suddenly Jay disappeared from view. Elise lowered her cell phone and zoomed. There was no Jay. It was as if he was swallowed up by the earth itself. She ran to the place where he just stood, thinking he had fallen in a sinkhole. The soil, though lose, was on solid ground.

Elise spoke up in a worried tone, "Jay if this is your idea of a joke, it's not funny!"

Time passed and still there was no answering call. Elise knew Jay, it wasn't like him to play mean tricks. She tramped through leaves and vines and paced back and forth across the clearing. She jumped when she heard the plaintive sound of a crow overhead.

Elise tried not to panic but fear rose in her voice as she called out, "Jay! Jay!"

She doubled back to the clearing and scanned the area again. She called Jay's name again and again. This time she heard a faint reply. The sound came from behind her. She raced back to the where the sandy soil was and scanned every inch of the area.

"Elise, I'm down here!" Jay yelled.

Elise ran to the sound and looked around. She noticed a deep depression under a flat overhanging moss-covered boulder. She crouched down to look and aimed her flashlight into the darkness. She gasped with relief when she spied Jay, 20 feet below, sprawled on the dirt floor of a hole.

She removed the nylon rope in her backpack, tied one end to a nearby tree and lowered herself down to Jay and exclaimed with relief, "Thank goodness! Are you hurt badly?" Tears sprang to her soft brown eyes as she helped him to his feet.

Jay held onto her arm and smiled, "I twisted my ankle but I don't think it's broken."

Elise hugged him, "I was so scared. I didn't think I would ever find you!"

Jay tried to stand, but wobbled against her-unable to put weight on his right foot without a shooting pain. Elise held onto him and gave him her water bottle. He drank thirstily from it and handed it back. Loose dirt and sweat dripped down his face. Elise took a moist wipe and gently cleaned him.

Elise looked up at him, "Do you think you can climb out of here?"

"Sure," Jay replied and added, "That's the easy part. I climb the vertical rope hand over hand in gym class every day for strength training. The walk back to the car will be the hard part."

"We'll find a strong tree branch and make a walking stick for you," Elise suggested.

Elise took her flashlight and scanned the deep hole around them and said, "Look, there are tunnels that branch off from here. You found an underground cave or den. Looks like some of the smaller tunnels were dug out by burrowing animals."

"That one to the right looks pretty wide," Jay observed. "I hope a black bear doesn't live here."

Elise turned and asked, "Do you hear that?"

"Hear what?" Jay stood still and listened, "The only thing I hear is the ringing in my ear. I boxed it when I fell. ."

"Jay be quiet and listen," Elise whispered. "Can't you hear that humming sound coming from the tunnel?"

"I do hear something now," Jay responded. "I hear the drumming sound of my heart telling me we need to get the hell out of here fast." When Elise gave him an irritated look, he nodded, "Yes, I hear a small buzzing sound like insects. Now can we go?"

Elise ignored him and yanked at his sleeve. "I have to see what's making that noise." She started down the tunnel and aimed the flashlight up ahead. She looked back at Jay. "Wait here I'll just take a look and come back."

Jay shook his head, "Are you crazy? What am I supposed to do while you're playing Indiana Jones?"

"Go ahead and climb out. Use the rope," Elise replied impatiently. "This is important. If that noise is what I think it is, we will get the highest grade on our report."

"Okay," Jay conceded. He struggled up the rope, grunted and mumbled under his breath, "I had to date Curious George's girl cousin!"

Elise continued down the larger tunnel to the right which twisted and turned a long way. The humming sound grew louder as she continued. After about ten minutes, she looked back, somewhat concerned about Jay.

Elise shook her head knowing that Jay would be okay and continued down the tunnel. The walls of the cave were rocky and slimy and bioluminescent moss or lichen covered them. Suddenly the tunnel swerved to the left and opened into a large chamber flooded with rays of sunlight from a small opening above.

Because her flashlight was no longer needed, she turned it off and gasped with wonder and awe at the scene up ahead. Realizing what it was, she was riveted to the scene, mesmerized by its strange beauty.

The walls were bathed in the eerier glow of glistening rainbow colors. The lichen grew from the floor of the ceiling until it touched sunlight and it stopped. Thousands of glistening honeycombs lined the walls of the cavern and continued into narrow tunnels branching off in all directions.

The humming sound was almost deafening so close to the main hive. Thousands of large honeybees flitted in and out of the chambers. They swiftly tended to the myriads of squirming larvae.

Without making a sound, Elise crept nearer to the heart of the hive. She scanned the honeycomb and found what she was looking for, the largest, plumpest queen bee she had ever seen. The queen lay on a soft mound of dirt in the center of the hive. Normal queens swelled up to two inches in length. This fertile mother was nearly 6 inches in length and the size of a goose egg. Her body rolled and bulged as it prepared to give birth to her brood.

Elise grabbed her cell phone and took a quick picture of the unbelievable scene. She quietly backed away from the hive. The tiny flash of light from her cell phone was instantaneous, but so were the queen's guardians when she was in danger. If she had alerted them they would send messages, communicate danger, swiftly mass, swarm in a buzzing cloud of anger and attack her.

As she was backed away, Elise noticed dead animals lay all around the floor of the cave near the hive. Their bellies were exposed and their bloated bodies were pock marked with tiny holes. She gasped as hundreds of bees spilled out of the holes and flew into the hive to feed the larvae. Other bees placed tissue matter into parts of the honeycomb to store for future use.

This was something she never seen before, bees feeding on mammals. Somehow the bees had mutated or evolved. She guessed that decades of pollution and danger caused some bees to move underground. They found other sources of food. Those colonies of bees not only survived but adapted to their new environment.

Elise took a video of the entire process. Her mind spun with the knowledge that this occurrence might change science and entomology forever!

The sound of the bees was deafening as Elise retreated back to the entrance of the hole. She imagined the frantic movements of millions of teeming bees in a cloud of deadly purpose jetting after her. Their tiny wings beating in a rapid blur as they flew in tandem. The queen's knights had one goal, to sting to death the enemy of their queen.

When Elise returned to the rope she climbed up as fast as she could, her heart raced and her breath came in gasps. The muscles of her legs and arms were strained with the effort and she tried not to cry out in pain. When she finally reached the edge of the hole, Jay pulled her up with his strong arms. She grabbed his hands with relief.

Elise looked at Jay and exclaimed, "What I saw in the cave was unbelievable!"

Jay helped her to her feet. He held her until she stopped trembling and said, "Jeeze Elise, are you okay?"

"I think so." Elise steadied her nerves and explained, "There huge cavern at the end of that tunnel." She pulled her stray auburn hair back into the ponytail and continued, "The walls were covered with a gigantic bee colony. As if all the colonies had somehow joined together for safety. Millions of bees were flying around tending to the honeycombs filled with eggs and larvae. The sound was so loud I thought I would go crazy." She touched the photo icon on her cell phone and showed Jay the pictures and the video she had taken.

Jay's brown eyes widened, he stared at the photo and exclaimed, "We better get out of here before they find us!"

They leaned on each other and made their way past the sandy soil to the clearing where they had eaten lunch earlier. Because of Jay's sprained ankle they were unable to move quickly, but they prodded on steadily to put as many miles as they could between them and the bees. They were relieved to hear no sounds of an impending swarm.

Jay stopped a moment to rest his leg and grinned over at Elise, "Mr. Henry will freak when he sees those photos. We should get an A+ for those alone."

They struggled through the thick undergrowth and pushed tangled branches aside. The sun was almost behind the trees, nearly at the horizon. Soon it would be dark and they would need their flashlights to continue.

Jay stopped and gazed at the red sky. He took a few breaths and looked at Elise, "I wonder why the bees went underground?"

"Maybe they are smarter about climate change than we are," Elise answered. "When their habitat above ground became too polluted, the colonies sent out an SOS and they all migrated to the cave."

"I don't buy it," Jay returned, "These woods don't look toxic to me. Why not just stay here above ground? No one here ruined their habitat, and the graph from 2 years ago doesn't show that all the colonies bugged out. There has to be a different reason this happened now."

Suddenly, the woods around them grew silent. No insects buzzed, no birds chirped, no animals scurried away from them as they move through the undergrowth. The air was eerily calm.

Jay and Elise turned to look, shielding their eyes from a bright white light that illuminated the southwestern sky. They heard a loud explosion in the distance, followed by violent tremors that knocked them to the ground. They held each other as the ear shattering sounds continued. After what seemed like hours, the earth stopped shaking. They sat up, clung to each other and waited.

The sky above them was bright red and dissolved into smoky gray. Then it lit up as if daylight had returned. The wind picked up as they rose to their feet.

Elise pointed to the western sky, "Jay look!"

Jay looked up and gasped, "I don't believe it! What just happened?"

The sky turned crimson, then orange then white. Turbulent winds swirled around them nearly knocking them back to the ground. They turned around bending against the wind and fled.

Just above the Ozark Mountain ridge it formed, blossomed and spread for miles. The giant mushroom cloud billowed and spread its poison over the earth.

Jay and Elise moved blindly as leaves and sticks and dirt swirled around them moved by the wind. They stumbled, fell and picked each other up.

Suddenly Elise turned north and shouted above the wind, "Back to the cave! We have to go underground."

"What about the bees?" Jay yelled back over the din.

"We'll have to take our chances," Elise replied supporting him and picking up the pace.

Deep within the cave, the bees had amassed around the queen. They gallantly cushioned her with their lives as the earth shook violently. Once the tremor ceased, they obediently went back to their work. Soon the queen would lay her eggs. After she let loose her brood, she would be ravenously hungry. She had to feed and store energy to survive the birthing.

The bee's strong bodies danced wildly, frantically sending messages throughout all the tunnels lined with massive honeycombs where other pregnant queens sheltered.

Their bodies began to vibrate and dance as they communicated the good news to the entire colony. Two warm-blooded beings had entered the cave. Their transmissions were received with joy. Food had arrived, food for their queen and their entire colony, food enough to last many lifetimes.

No Place For
A Woman

No Place for a Woman

M edic, Maria Torres, nodded to Sgt. Pete Russo as they bumped along in the medical supply truck on a wind blasted desert road in Afghanistan. They were transporting much needed medical supplies to Sector 7's temporary Army hospital.

Sgt. Russo returned her nod and commented, "This frigging war is no place for a woman."

Suddenly, a deafening explosion rocked the vehicle. The driver was catapulted into the windshield and bounced back with a crash. When he finally landed against the steering wheel, his body hung limp and lifeless.

As the truck skidded and tumbled on its side, turned upside down, and rolled over and over, Maria was tossed like a pea in a tin can. She was flung into the front seat and landed on Sgt. Russo, whose head lolled to the right. A gash on his forehead gushed blood and an egg-sized purple bruise began to form.

The vehicle finally stopped with an ear shattering jolt as it slammed into the rocky wall of an abandoned well. Maria reached past the driver and turned off the engine. The wheels stopped their maniacal spinning and the truck finally stood still.

Maria took a deep breath and checked herself for injuries. She was badly bruised and shaken but still in one piece.

She checked Sgt. Russo and was relieved to discover he was unconscious but alive. Sgt. Sean Casey, their driver was not so lucky. Maria bowed her head in resignation as she discovered that he had mercifully died on impact. She savagely pulled the keys from the ignition and wept.

When heavy smoke poured from under the bent and sprung hood of the truck, Maria went into action. She pulled at Russo's body and dragged him over the seat which had flatten to the back in the crash. She pulled and tugged Russo toward the back of the truck. She opened the interior supply door and eased his body onto the floor. She gritted her teeth as her muscles, stretched to the breaking point and knotted up with pain.

Maria scrambled in the hold and recovered Medic Deran Jackson from under the heavy boxes of supplies that had fallen in the crash. His youthful brown face was mottled with shards of broken glass. The two small side windows on the van had burst inward as the vehicle rolled over. Jackson's left arm hung at a crazy angel. She sighed with relief to find his pulse was weak but steady.

She jumped out the back door of the truck and carefully removed both men and laid them on the ground away from the smoking vehicle. After what seemed like hours she dragged them both to safety behind the stone wall of the abandoned well.

Maria pulled a rag over her face and sprinted back to the burning truck. She filled her pack with medical supplies and the first aid kit. She dropped the pack next to the men and returned to the truck. She had to retrieve as many of the medical supplies as she could. She dashed back and forth to the truck and loading supplies into a plastic container and emptying them into the dry well.

Her knuckles were bruised and bleeding from bumping the bent doors of the truck on the way out. She wiped them with gauze and sat down next to the men. She watched as the truck caught fire.

Maria ascertained that the road side bomb had been poorly constructed or all of them would have perished. She stood up, but before she could return to the truck to retrieve Casey's body, the gas tank exploded. Maria hit the dirt and covered the two wounded men with her body. Thankfully the massive stones of the abandoned well had shielded them from harm.

With one last blast the explosions ceased and the earth stopped shaking. Looking around for a place to hide the men and secure their position, Maria spotted an abandoned dwelling in the distance.

Maria took a long drink from her water bottle and examined the wounded men. Russo needed stitches but she carefully placed a loose bandage on his head wound. Jackson's arm looked broken but not too badly. She took a large roll of gauze and wrapped it round and round and secured his injured arm to his body. Now that the men were stabilized, it was imperative that she move their bodies to the shelter.

The hot sun glared mercilessly down on them. Without shelter they would quickly dehydrate. None of them would last very long. She had noticed that the radio in the truck was smashed and unusable. It was up to her to keep them all alive until help came.

After nearly two hours, she finally was able to drag the two injured men into the shelter. The roof was still intact at one end and there was enough shade to give them blessed relief from the sun.

Both men were unconscious but she managed to wet their faces with water and cool them off. She hoped that the explosion had been seen by one of the helicopters that scanned the area. She also knew that the explosion could attract the enemy as well. Maria checked her rifle, relieved to find it was still in working condition. She had an extra clip of ammunition in her bag just in case.

She took one of the 4 army blankets she had stuffed in her duffel bag and draped it over the only window to stifle the afternoon heat.

She scrubbed her hands with a sanitizing wipe, opened the first aid kit and knelt over the wounded men. On further inspection, she discovered that Jackson's arm was not broken but dislocated. He was still out cold when she tugged on his lower arm braced the upper arm and heard the sickening crunch that meant she had put his arm back in place. His face contorted in pain and she administered an injection of pain killer.

She deftly removed at least 20 shards of glass from the side of his face. They bled freely but none were too deep. She cleaned the area with antibacterial wipes and bandaged his entire cheek and part of his forehead.

Maria gasped when she examined the rest of Jackson's body. After she carefully removed his jacket, she discovered a small piece of metal from the side of the truck had pierced his side. The shard was lodged between two ribs but no arteries appeared to be nicked or severed. She cleaned the area with antiseptic but left the shrapnel alone. If she removed he could bleed to death. A surgeon would have to tend to that wound.

Russo's wound looked worse than it was. The gash was not as deep as she feared but the bruise was swelling more. There was a cold pack in her kit and she gently laid that on the bump. She took a butterfly bandage, closed the gash and covered it with loose fitting gauze in case he had a concussion. She lifted his eyelids and discovered his pupils were slightly different from each other.

Maria sat back and looked over at the two men with worry. Both of them needed more professional care than she could give. Jackson's wounds could become infected in hours, and Russo could lapse into a coma. She injected them both with an antibiotic but the dose would wear off fast.

What worried Maria the most was the weird indentation in Russo's temple. She knew that could be fatal if he had a subdural bruise. She checked his pupils again and sighed. She would have to see if she could wake Pete up before he never woke up.

"Russo!'" she exclaimed. She shook his body. She massaged his arms and legs and called his name again. "Pete, wake up!"

She continued talking to him, massaging his body and shaking him gently. Finally out of frustration she yelled into his ear, "Come on Pete! You told me you were a hard-headed Sicilian, now prove it!"

When her attempts to awaken him were unsuccessful, she collapsed against the wall and tried to force back tears of anger and frustration. She pulled the window shade aside and watched as the fiery sun sunk below the horizon. It would bring relief from the heat, but with it came the biting cold of the desert night. The temperature could drop below 40 degrees.

As the cold wind whipped the makeshift cover on the window, Maria took out the remaining blankets from her pack. She covered the 2 men with them and placed a silver emergency blanket over that. It would hold in their body heat and keep them warm.

Maria moved toward the crumbling doorway of the hovel and gazed out onto the moonlit terrain. She used her rifle's scope to scan the area for any sign of the enemy. She pulled her jacket closed and blew on her cold hands.

Exhausted, dirty and helpless she said aloud, "Where are the damned choppers? They must know we are missing by now!" She shook her head a and murmured, "This must be what hell is like, hot as fire in the daytime and cold as ice at night"

Maria gazed up at the full moon. It stared down at her like a glaring Cyclops. A myriad of stars twinkled coldly like thousands of loveless eyes.

In the distance she heard the pop, pop, pop of gunfire. She told herself it was probably a night raid on some war-torn, blasted out, desolate, rundown wreck of what passed for a town in this part of the world. She could imagine terrified mothers, huddled in the dark and cold, cradling their babies in their arms while their men fought endlessly to protect them. In the midst of all this madness were U.S. troops ordered to make peace with guns and grenades.

Maria wondered if Russo was right. Perhaps she was trying to prove that a woman could make a difference in this unending war against terrorism. She had joined the military after she earned her RN to save lives.

She swallowed caffeine tablets throughout the night to stay awake. Around 2am she heard a noise. Something was snuffling around in the darkness. She peered out the window and saw the outline of an animal, a lone scavenger that foraged for food. Maria crept outside, picked up a large stone and hefted it at the animal. It yelped loudly and scampered away.

Dawn came early and with it scorching heat. At 7am it was already oppressively hot. Tired and blurry eyed Maria checked on the men. Jackson moved restlessly. His eyes flickered a moment and he gave her a weak smile. He groaned loudly as she gave him a drink of water and a small dose of pain meds. His expression softened as he drifted off to sleep.

Russo was still out cold. She checked his pupils relieved to see they were uniform. His pulse was strong and the swelling on his head had gone down. Maria massaged his arms and legs to keep his circulation flowing and spoke to him a bantering tone, "Come on Pete, wake up! Do I have to do all the work? Give a woman a break!"

A sob broke from Maria's throat and unchecked tears streamed down her sweaty cheeks. She liked Pete Russo. He was like a big brother to her, even if he was a chauvinist. She let go of his hand and tried to calm herself.

"Oh God, where are the choppers," Maria whispered to herself, then added, "The men can't stand another day in this heat, not with their wounds as bad as they are. Did we survive the IED only to die in this God-forsaken desert?"

She shook her head and willed herself to shake off her rising fear. The men needed her and she would keep them alive, if it killed her. She had to laugh at that crazy thought.

"Hey Pete, I'm losing it!" she said. She looked down at him and froze. His eyelids fluttered a few seconds.

Sgt. Pete Russo opened his dark brown eyes and in a hoarse voice asked, "Roadside bomb get us?" When Maria nodded he continued, "Anyone killed?"

Maria squeezed his hand, "Casey didn't make it." Seeing Pete's stricken look she added, "I don't think he suffered, it was instant."

He twisted his head painfully and looked over at Jackson. "Is he okay?"

"He's stable," Maria answered, "Jackson took some shrapnel. He'll need a surgeon."

Pete grimaced, "Help coming?"

"The radio is busted," Maria answered. "They have to know we are lost by now. It's been over 12 hours since we were supposed to drop off the supplies."

"Did we lose them too?" Pete asked.

"No!" Maria answered, "I got them out and stowed them in

an empty well right before the truck blew! The supplies are safely hidden. It's cool and dry down there."

Pete gave her a "thumbs up" sign and said, "Quick thinking!"

Maria smiled down at him, "You should have seen me racing back and forth like I was in an Olympic relay race!"

Pete laughed weakly, "And I know how you hate running."

They both laughed as Maria handed him a bottle of fresh water. She gently lifted his head so he could take a drink.

Russo grimaced, touched his head and exclaimed, "Ouch!"

"Hey! Stop that!" Maria ordered in a warning tone. "Finally, I get some pay back for all that teasing. Now I can truly say you are a big sore head."

They were still laughing when they heard the familiar sound of helicopter rotors. Maria looked out the window and grinned. She raced from the shelter and waved her arms.

She turned back and yelled into the little stone hovel, "Hey Russo, it's ours!"

The Medivac chopper landed 30 yards away and kicked up a whirlwind of dirt. Soldiers and medics poured out of the helicopter and sprinted towards her. Maria pointed to the shelter. She showed the pilot where the medical supplies were.

Once safely aboard and in the air, Maria sat between Jackson and Russo on the way to the hospital. One medic examined them and the other made a call to the medical staff at the base to prepare them for the incoming wounded.

Maria smiled down at Pete. He looked up at her and winked. She squeezed his hand and asked, "Now what were you saying about women and this war?"

Russo grinned up at her and answered, "I was saying there's no way in hell we can win without them!"

Gentle Breeze Resort

Gentle Breeze Resort

The five weary travelers motored down the narrow two lane country highway. Only the SUV's headlights illuminated the dark road ahead. A golden harvest moon hung over the coniferous forest casting a glow on the Ozark Mountain ridge.

Nancy yawned, gripped the wheel with one hand and took a gulp of black coffee with the other. Her fiancé, Dean, slept on with his head on her shoulder.

Dean had instructed her to make a right turn on highway Z. Nancy checked the GPS on her cell phone and saw the he was correct. Their destination, Gentle Breeze Resort, was fifteen miles down Highway Z.

As she swerved onto Z, Dean's brother, Daniel, and his wife, Tanya slumbered peacefully in the back seat. Their dog, Sparky, a shepherd terrier mix, was curled up on the floor. He snored softly as his paws twitched amid dreams of chasing squirrels.

Highway Z was a winding road with rolling rises and steep slopes and rounded curves that meandered sharply to right and left. Nancy's stomach lurched as if she were riding on a roller coaster at Six Flags Amusement Park. She slowed down from 70 to 50 for better control. Racing on narrow roads at midnight was not her idea of fun.

On a slight strait away she took another drink of coffee. It wasn't surprising she was all worn out. On impulse, Dean suggested they hike the eight miles up the Apple Wood Mountain trail to

Eagle Point Lookout Tower which overlooked a beautiful Ozark Mountain valley.

As they stood on the lookout terrace, majestic eagles and hawks had soared above them in the cloudless azure skies. When they looked down at the valley below they had spied a deer family drinking from the silvery waters of a snaking river. They quickly captured the moments on their cell phones and shared their photos.

Nancy left her reveries and cruised along at a moderate speed. Highway Z had finally calmed down its crazy twists and turns. She checked the GPS and happily discovered that they were less than 3 miles from Gentle Breeze Resort.

Dean had warned her about the deer trails in the area but she wasn't prepared for the huge 10 point buck that leaped out of the forest and ran in front of the car. Nancy turned the wheel and swerved off the road to avoid the magnificent animal.

The deer bounded away unscathed and Nancy pumped the breaks as the SUV careened downward. The car's headlights illuminated the terrain as she frantically turned the wheel to avoid the trees.

The bumping and bouncing of the car jerked everyone awake. Dean yelled and took hold of the steering wheel to help Nancy control the car. Sparky howled in terror behind the seat. Daniel and Tanya cried out as their seat belts and harnesses knocked them painfully back in their seats.

Nancy slammed on the brakes. She and the others watched in horror as the SUV picked up speed. As they careened down the hill out of control, branches and vines scraped the sides and hood of the car. Low tree branches caught and ripped off the windshield wipers. The headlights took a beating and the front end was scraped and dented.

A giant oak, captured in the head lights, loomed directly ahead of them. Thankfully, the terrain leveled out. Nancy pressed the pedal and turned the wheel to avoid the massive trunk of an ancient oak.

Mercifully, they avoided the tree and the SUV finally came to a halt at the bottom of the ravine. Nancy put the car in park and turned off the engine.

Dean gathered Nancy into his arms. "Are you okay?" he asked in a worried tone.

Nancy gasped and took a deep breath, "I'm fine. There was a deer!" Nancy looked at him and sobbed, "I'm sorry I wrecked the car."

Dean looked into her eyes, "It's okay honey. You did your best."

From the back seat Tanya commented, "You did good girlfriend! We're alive and in one piece."

"Well, I guess we're taking another hike," Daniel commented drolly as he handed the girls their backpacks.

The two couples took out their flashlights and hiked back to the country road. The summer air was satiny cool and smoothed their frayed nerves.

Sparky wagged his tail and trotted ahead. He stopped to sniff and mark each bush, just in case he had to find his way back to the car.

Tanya laughed at the dog's antics commenting, "At least Sparky is having fun."

After they walked a few miles, the group rounded a bend in the road. They shouted in relief when they saw the sign posted on a gated entrance, "Gentle Breeze Resort-One Mile." When they got within a few feet of the ornate wrought iron entrance, the gate opened with a noisy creaking sound.

Daniel looked at Tanya, "Spooky! What's with the haunted mansion sounds? I thought this was an elegant modern resort nestled in the foot hills of the Ozarks, like the brochure said. Instead we got a rusty rickety old gate that needs a gallon of oil!"

Dean laughed and commented, "The brochure was probably bogus and we wasted our money. Let's hope they have a tractor to pull the car out of the ravine."

"Hopefully not pulled by two old gray nags," Daniel added. Tanya reached over and pinched his arm. "Ouch!" he replied in faux pain.

The gravel road was lit by a series of old fashioned gaslights that led them to a cobblestone circle drive. The main lodge was a huge looming monstrosity. Two tall towers with stone turrets pierced the moonlit sky on either side. Tulip shaped stone cornices decorated each of the three floors and grimacing gargoyles jutted over the portcullis.

Above the entrancen, tall beveled windows gleamed in the moonlight. An elegant gas light fixture of fluted lilies illuminated a wrap-around porch. Two huge red oak doors marked the entrance to the resort.

Nancy climbed the stone stairs and said, "Cancel our account with "Best Kept Travel Secrets".

Tanya agreed, "Best keep it a secret too!"

Daniel groaned and stated, "Maybe we can get our money back."

Tanya took his hand and asked, "Come on Danny, where is your sense of adventure?"

Daniel shook his head and exclaimed, "I left it back in the ditch where we almost hit that tree and got splattered all over the forest!"

Nancy looked up at the grotesque structure and leaned toward Dean, "Maybe they should call this place, "Gothic Hideaway" instead of Gentle Breeze Resort."

Dean looked up at the gargoyles, "More like, Mr. Hyde's Country Manor."

As they paused in front of the massive doors, they heard a plaintive sound. It came from Sparky. He sat rigidly at the bottom of the stairs.

"Sparky come here sweetie," Tanya coaxed.

Sparky looked up at her with dark eyes and refused to move. He snuffled and whined and bent his head.

Daniel gazed down at the dog, "Don't dogs have a sixth sense about danger? Maybe he's trying to tell us to get the hell out of here as fast as we can."

"He does keep looking into the woods like he'd rather be there," Nancy remarked.

"He's just nervous like us," Tanya said.

Dean took Nancy's hand and they waited on the top of the

stairs. The huge porch loomed in both directions. High-backed rocking chairs rocked gently in the breeze. Several wooden porch swings swayed back and forth as if they held ghostly couples romancing in the moonlight.

Dean grabbed the huge Lion's head door knocker banged it down and said, "I think we just warped back to a scene from "A Christmas Carol".

"The whole place is definitely Dickensian," Tanya commented.

One massive door opened and a charming lady in her fifties dressed in a navy blue uniform complete with a perky ruffled cap greeted them.

"Welcome, we were expecting you. I'm Mrs. Walden, the housekeeper." Behind Mrs. Walden a thin young woman in a similar uniform, curtsied. "This is Nell, the upstairs maid. Come in. Come in. You're the first guests to arrive. I expect the other four couples will arrive later tonight. This is an annual visit for them."

Dean nodded and explained, "Good to meet you. We left our suitcases back in the car. We had a bit of an accident and our car ended up in a gully about four miles back."

Mrs. Walden put her hand to her neck and said, "Was it a deer?" She sighed and continued, "That old buck causes at least three or four accidents a year. We call him, King. Gaming rules forbid anyone to hunt him because the resort is on state park lands.

Nell gave Dean a sympathetic look, "Don't worry about your car, sir. My husband, Jack, will bring the tractor around and pull it out of the ditch and bring back your luggage."

"Thank you," Dean replied.

Mrs. Walden led them into a spacious receiving room. It was opulently decorated with tasteful Early American and French inspired furniture.

Nancy and Tanya surveyed the elegant room. They paused and admired the Mahogany sideboard that was set against mauve-painted wall. The portrait of a handsome man in old fashioned attire was mounted in an ornate golden frame hung above the sideboard.

The dining table was a dark walnut and decorated with a large oval silver terrine filled with roses. Above the table was a simple glass and brass chandelier with crystal etched-tulip shaped bulb covers.

The Queen Anne sofa and love seat in the large drawing room were upholstered in a muted cabbage rose design with green leaves. Dark hardwood floors gleamed in the soft light. Large mauve ginger jar lamps sat on the side tables. The tables had white and gray veined marble tops and carved walnut stands. Lovely area rugs in shades of rose and mauve warmed the room.

Dean and Daniel admired the huge carved wooden chess set in black and white that stood in front of two tall multi-paned beveled windows. The chess pieces were over 3 feet high. The king and queen's golden crowns were bejeweled with sparkling green and red crystals.

Dean hoisted the black bishop piece by its gold leafed clergy hat. To his surprise it wasn't very heavy. Apparently the pieces were hollow inside. Daniel moved the King piece and said, "Checkmate! Bow to your king!"

Mrs. Walden walked over and smiled, "Fifty years ago, a local Osage Native American crafted each chess piece from hollowed out tree trunks. The Millers owned the resort in those days. Please have a seat. Your luggage should be here shortly."

Nell brought a tray of fruit and cheeses into the room and placed it on the sideboard. She smiled and left with a slight curtsy. She returned a minute later with a silver tray with a bottle of Port and crystal wine glasses and placed it on the tatted lace runner.

Mrs. Walden nodded to Nell, "Thank you Nell. I'll serve our guests."

Nancy gazed over at the gilt framed portrait over the side table. The slender young man wore a quilted burgundy jacket and black riding pants. He held an ornate riding crop with an ivory carved handle sporting and eagles head.

"That is a portrait of the original owner of Gentle Breeze Manor, Jeffrey Damen III," Mrs. Walden offered. "He was a dashing young man in his time, the most eligible bachelor in Southwest

Missouri. He commissioned the family estate in 1904. Magnificent balls and social evenings were held here throughout the year. The wealthy landowners, farmers and local population were all invited."

"He certainly was handsome," Tanya added. "Like a prince from a fairy tale."

Mrs. Walden nodded as she poured the wine, "He didn't stay a bachelor for long. He met his wife, Jasmine, on a buying trip to India in 1908. She was a daughter of a wealthy merchant and a cousin of the caliph."

Nancy gazed at the portrait again, "That must have been a struggle, not only to win Jasmine from her family but for her to be accepted here."

"It was a challenge," Mrs. Walden agreed, "but I believe Mr. Damen bought some land in Ceylon her family coveted and gave it to his future father-in-law. Jasmine was released with her family's blessing and brought quite a dowry to the marriage. You can see Jasmine's portrait on the landing when you go up the stairs to your rooms."

Tanya gazed at the portrait at the top of the stairs, took a sip of her wine and put the glass down and asked, "I wonder what Jasmine was like?"

"From family diaries and history, I take it she was as kind as she was beautiful," Mrs. Walden answered, "She and Jeffery were very much in love. Because of her beauty, and giving nature, the people adored her. She would visit them with gifts for birthdays, newborns or just to chat about local flowers and vegetables."

"Did they have children?" Nancy inquired.

"They had two sons, Samuel and Ned, beautiful dark-haired boys with flashing brown eyes," Mrs. Walden said with a faraway look in her moist eyes.

"From your expression I take it things did not end well for them," Dean offered.

Mrs. Walden nodded and explained, "One winter a terrible contagion spread through the region. The fever quickly reached the tenant farmers. Jasmine was trained in the homeopathic cures of her Indian heritage, and offered to nurse the sick. The epidemic ravaged the countryside for over a year and finally burned itself out."

Mrs. Walden was nearly in tears as she continued, "Not soon enough for poor Jasmine though. She took ill and died two days before Christmas, that was 1920."

Daniel poured another glass of wine and commented, "The flu Pandemic of 1918 killed thousands in America and all over the world. Even President Wilson got sick."

"What happened to Jeffrey?" Nancy asked.

Mrs. Walden dabbed her eyes with a handkerchief and explained, "Jeffery was so devastated that he took to his rooms and wasn't seen for months. He hired an English Nanny to take care of the boys who were 5 and 7. He sent the boys to boarding school in the East two years later. After that he became a recluse. He haunted this place for another thirty years."

"And the children, what became of them?" Tanya asked.

"Samuel and Ned came home for holidays but less and less over the years," Mrs. Walden replied, "Both son's joined the army as officers and fought in World War II. They managed to survive, only to come home and bury their father. They sold the estate to the Millers, went back east became very wealthy businessmen and never returned."

Nancy and Tanya looked at the portrait of Jeffery Damon III and then at each other. Both had felt something strange when they gazed into the handsome man's eyes.

Tanya looked up at Mrs. Walden. She dabbed her mouth with her napkin and asked, "Mrs. Walden, is Gentle Breeze haunted?"

Mrs. Walden's looked over at Tanya with raised eyebrows, "With the manor's history, I would be surprised if it weren't."

Tanya and Nancy exchanged glances. Dean and Daniel suppressed grins and sipped their wine.

"Now I'll leave all of you in peace," Mrs. Walden announced, "Enjoy the rest of your snack. Nell we return soon to show you to your rooms. If you need anything before bed let her know. The kitchen closes at 10pm."

"Thank you for the family history," Nancy replied.

Mrs. Walden gave her a nod and a slight smile, "I'll see you in the morning."

Dean nibbled at a cheese straw and took a sip of wine. He saw Nancy's serious expression and patted her arm, "Nancy, I know you love a mystery but don't take Mrs. Walden too seriously."

Daniel let out a laugh. "I'm sorry Nance but you should see your face. You look like you've just seen a ghost or something!"

Tanya gave him a dark look, "Hey don't make fun of her. I felt something too."

When Nell walked into the room from the shadows without a sound and they all jumped. She smiled and stated, "The rooms are ready for you. Just follow me up the stairs."

Tanya paused a moment and turned to Daniel, "Get Sparky will you?"

"Okay you go on up and I'll meet you there." Daniel agreed.

When the trio reached the landing they paused to look at the large portrait of Jasmine Damon. She was strikingly beautiful. Her long black tresses were pulled back and wrapped in Jasmine flowers. She was dressed in straight flapper style gown in dark blue with silver sequins in a starry pattern. A wispy scarf of silvery material covered her tawny brown shoulders. A long pearl necklace hung to her waist. Dark blue gloves covered her slender hands and forearms. She wore elegant glass slippers with Louis heels on her slender feet. Jasmine stood on a smooth flagstone patio. Behind her, Lilac bushes, Jasmine and Cardinal Bushes bloomed from a terra cotta bordered garden. In the background farmlands, pine trees and the foothills of the Ozarks created a pastoral scene.

The trio continued up the next flight of stairs to their rooms. Nancy turned to Tanya as they paused on the landing and whispered, "What a gorgeous woman Jasmine was."

Tanya nodded "What a loss it must have been for her family and all the people who loved her."

Dean looked over at the two women with a grin and asked, "Why are you two whispering?"

Tanya gave him a puzzled look, "It's this house!" When Nancy nodded her head in agreement, she continued, "It makes you feel humble and small. Like there is something here out of the ordinary, special, you know?"

Dean wiggled his fingers and laughed, "We don't want to wake the restless spirits that walk these halls!"

Nell, who waited patiently for them in the hall, looked at Dean and said, "This room is yours sir," she motioned to Tanya "The one across the hall is yours."

"Thank you Nell," Dean said.

"Will there be anything else?" Nell inquired.

Tanya gave her a worried look, "Just check on Daniel and Sparky for me, will you?"

"Of course I'll be happy to," Nell replied. She smiled gave a slight curtsy and headed back down the stairs.

"She was trained by the British no doubt," Nancy commented as they watched Nell's quiet retreat down the stairs.

"I think it's sweet, as if she comes from a different era," Tanya commented.

As they opened the door to their rooms, they heard footsteps on the stairs. Daniel had returned carrying Sparky.

"What's the matter with Sparky?" Tanya asked petting the shaking dog.

Daniel gave the dog to Tanya, "I have no idea. He was fine when he ran over to me and raced up the stairs. When he got to the porch he whined and trembled like he was scared and refused to come in. I had to pick him up!"

Tanya petted Sparky and looked into his large brown eyes. She held him by the cheeks and kissed the top of his head, "It's okay, sweetie. We won't let anything happen to you."

Sparky wagged his tail hopefully and Tanya and Daniel entered their room.

Across the hall Nancy and Dean paused at the door. Dean took Nancy into his arms, "Are you okay with us sharing the same room?"

Nancy laughed and kissed him, "You are an old fashioned guy

at heart but we're engaged! In three weeks we will be married. I think we can risk it."

Dean opened the door and they entered the bedroom, "Nice room."

The elegant room was spacious and inviting. The floor to ceiling windows had beveled glass panes which held richly-hued royal blue brocade drapes. The walls were papered with a tiny cornflower design.

The long Mahogany dresser against the left wall gleamed with brass handles and was protected with a cream beige-colored lace runner. Above the dresser, a tri-paneled French inspired gold leafed framed mirror was hung. On either side of the mirror Art Deco inspired sconces illuminated the room.

On the opposite wall between two beveled windows was an antique queen sized four-poster bed complete with bed drapes in Cornflower blue to match the hand sewn quilt. The marble topped tables that stood on either side of the magnificent bed, held beautiful Tiffany Lamps with hummingbirds and fluted Lily designs.

A Queen Anne love seat sat in front of the tall windows. In the right corner was a Mahogany Closet and a tall Chest of Drawers that matched the dresser stood in the left corner.

The highly polished hardwood floors were warmed with decorative area rugs in cornflower blue.

"It's beautiful!" Nancy said she twirled around the room in delight.

"This must be the blue room the brochure highlighted," Dean commented. He walked to the windows and scanned the grounds. "What a fantastic view! Look! There's a tennis court on the right!"

Nancy joined him and exclaimed, "Take a look to the left. That looks like an old fashioned hedge maze!"

Dean looked to the left, "Now that is worth seeing. I've been through a hay bale maze in Kimswick when I was a kid but never one with bushes 8 feet all!"

Tanya tapped on the door walked into their room, "Lovely room. It's the same layout as ours."

Daniel knocked and poked his head in the room, "We have the green room. Everything is decorated in shades of forest green. Our luggage is out in the hall by the way. Nell's husband, Jack, creeped up here a few minutes ago and Sparky nearly had a heart attack!"

Tanya pulled Daniel into the hall, "Well, goodnight." She turned to Daniel, "We better let Sparky out before bed."

Daniel waved to Dean and Tanya, "Sleep tight you all. Don't let the ghostly bed bugs bite!"

"Sweet Dreams," Nancy said laughing.

"You get ready for bed, hon," Daniel took the dog's leash, "I'll let goofy out!"

After Dean and Nancy went to bed they turned down the lamps and gazed out the window at the harvest moon. Puffy clouds rolled by and hid its soft glow for a few moments.

Nancy got out of bed and walked over to the windows, "Dean, come and look."

Dean joined her at the window. When he looked out he saw an animal flitting across the moonlit grass, "That looks like Sparky!"

"Dean, should we go get him?" Nancy asked with a worried look on her face.

Dean replied, "I'm sure Tanya and Daniel know he's out there. He'll come back. That dog was born under a wondering star. He's always running off somewhere."

Daniel took her hand and led her to their bed and said, "Come on honey, we should get some sleep."

Nancy lay next to Dean and he enveloped her in his arms. The room was flooded with soft moonlight. She turned to look at his lightly tanned face, caressed his brown hair and said softly, "I can't wait until we're married."

Dean kissed her softly and held her close, "Three weeks love, and we won't ever sleep alone again."

In moments, the room disappeared and there was only the two of them wrapped in the warmth of love.

Morning came and with it the sound of a cock crowing in the distance. Bright sunbeams pierced through the windows and danced on their faces.

Nancy stretched luxuriously and headed for the bathroom. It was easily the size of Nancy's whole bedroom in St. Louis. It was all in white, the walls the fixtures and the curtains. It was like walking into a cloud. She stepped off the cold tile and onto the large plush rug in front of the tub and ran a warm bath. She poured in a few drops of the rose scented bath oil on the counter and waited for the tub to fill.

She gazed into the mirror over the vanity and smiled at herself. A feeling of contentment surrounded her. Soft honey colored curls surrounded her heart-shaped face and trailed down her smooth back.

The room was bathed with such bright white light that in the mirror she looked almost transparent. She shook off the strange feeling that had suddenly driven her smile away and stepped into the tub.

Dean tapped on the door and Nancy invited him in. He stood at the mirror and shaved while she sang to herself surrounded by mountains of bubbles.

"Hand me a towel," Nancy said as she rose from the tub.

Dean grinned at her and stated, "Better put your robe on quick, girl or I might grab you and we'll be late for breakfast."

Nancy wrapped herself into her plush pink bathrobe and kissed him as she went out the door into the other room.

While Dean was showering, Nancy got dressed. She chose a white peasant blouse over a Navy swing skirt decorated with white daisies. Her silky long hair flowed down her back. She slipped on white sandals and applied pink gloss to her lips.

She surveyed herself in the antiqued mirrors and smiled. The outfit gave her a turn of the century country girl appearance. She smiled and pulled the white crocheted shawl her grandmother had made for her for Christmas on her shoulders.

Dean wrapped the large bath towel around his body and watched Nancy twirl around in her lovely skirt. He walked up to her and whistled, "You look ravishing, me-lady."

Nancy laughed, "You better get dressed sweet prince before I pull that towel off of you!"

"We could skip breakfast," Dean said with a come hither look.

"Not on your life," Nancy replied, "I just got dressed and I'm starving!"

Dean quickly dressed in a light blue cotton shirt and navy slacks. He grinned at Nancy's startled look and commented, "What? You want me to wear my usual, running pants and white T-shirt?"

"No!" Nancy exclaimed, "You look very suave."

"When I saw how great you looked I had to do something different," Dean commented, "besides, this house is a mansion not a spa."

Tanya and Daniel emerged from their rooms dressed in equal finery. Tanya wore a fitted sky blue sheath and matching princess slippers. Her dark hair floated around her lovely brown face down to her shoulders. Daniel wore a white cotton shirt and brown chinos.

Nancy looked at Tanya and asked, "Did Sparky ever come back? Dean and I looked out the windows and saw him running on the grounds last night."

"He certainly did," Tanya replied, "that pesky dog was howling at the front door at 2 am."

As they walked down the stairs Nell appeared and said, "Good Morning, I hope you slept well. Breakfast will be served on the patio this morning."

Tanya smiled at her, "Good morning to you. Sorry about our dog making such a fuss last night." She turned to Dean and asked, "Dean, will you get Sparky? He can sit outside with us."

Nell escorted them through the patio doors and seated them at a white wooden table. As they sat down Nancy looked over at Tanya and exclaimed "Look it's just like the patio in Jasmine's portrait!"

"What a beautiful garden," Tanya replied, "I can smell the Jasmine."

Daniel joined them with Sparky who was very happy to sit right under the table waiting for any tidbits of bacon or any other breakfast foods that might accidentally fall on the flagstone within his reach.

Nell returned with coffee and served all around. She reached under the table and petted Sparky saying, "I'll bring a bowl and some bacon rinds and such for you."

Tanya grinned at her, "Thank you so much, Nell. You know the way to Sparky's heart."

Beyond the patio and past the flowering bushes a stone fountain with flying fish sprayed water on wading herons. At the apex of the fountain, a beautiful statue of a young girl stood holding a large jug that poured a stream of water into the lower basin.

As Tanya and Nancy discussed the gardens and statuary, Dean and Daniel eyed the tennis courts in the distance.

"If we are going to play tennis we should do it early," Daniel pointed out to Dean, "It feels like it's going to be a scorcher today."

Dean gave him a thumb's up as he sipped his coffee, "I'm not going to let you win this time, brother."

Daniel laughed, "In your dreams!"

When Nell returned with a fresh carafe of coffee, Nancy asked, "Nell where are the other guests?"

Nell suppressed a yawn, "They arrived early this morning, ma'am. They are probably sleeping."

Tanya smiled up at Nell, "You poor lady. First Sparky wakes up the whole house and then guests! You must be exhausted."

Nell finished filling their cups, "I'm sure they'll be down for the evening meal. They're regulars and we get used to their unusual schedule. In the meantime you have the whole resort to yourselves for the day, enjoy."

Nancy touched Tanya's arm and asked, "What about a nice swim and some girl time while the guys play tennis?"

Tanya nodded, "Sounds like a plan, girlfriend!"

While the two men set off with Sparky to play tennis the girls spent the early afternoon swimming, sipping ice tea and chatting. After an hour, Tanya, put on her sandals, grabbed her cover-up and said, "Look, Nancy, Sparky is off on another junket!"

Nancy looked past the tennis courts and saw Sparky as he disappeared down the path into the woods. She threw on her cover-up and sandals and said, "Let's see where he's going."

After a mile they saw that the path meandered behind the hedge maze. The maze was enclosed by a wrought iron fence and was secured with a heavily locked gate.

Tanya looked over at Nancy, "Look at the size of that lock!"

"What are they protecting in there?" Nancy said. She read the metal sign on the gate, "Off limits to guests."

Tanya gave Nancy a puzzled look, "I wonder why it's off limits. I know the guys would love to get us lost in that thing!"

"Maybe someone did get lost in there," Nancy offered.

Tanya looked at her with wide eyes, "Or maybe someone got lost and disappeared!"

"That would cause quite a scandal," Nancy commented.

Suddenly, Sparky sprang out of one of the maze corridors, startling both women. He easily squeezed through the wrought iron bars of the gate.

"That's the terrier in him," Tanya said, "They can squeeze through anything they can get their nose in!" She bent down and petted the dog, who promptly slurped her face. She shook her head and added, "Sparky, you scared us to death! Did you solve the maze?"

Sparky looked up at his mistress but before she could grab his collar he streaked off again. This time he sprinted down the road toward the entrance gates.

Nancy grabbed her friend's sleeve, "Come on Tanya we'll never catch up with him. He'll turn up later when he gets hungry."

Tanya sighed, "You're probably right. He's really having the time of his life. Sparky has an uncanny ability to show up at meal times no matter when they are."

When they arrived at the tennis courts the men had just finished a third set. They walked off the court mopped off their sweat-drenched faces and waved to the girls.

Dean sat down at the picnic table and sighed, "I let my little brother win two out of three."

Daniel laughed, "That's right bro! You're 6 years older than me. Maybe you're just getting old!"

They sat down with the girls and were told about Sparky's adventure and the keep out sign at the maze.

Dean looked over at Daniel, "That sounds like a challenge to me. What about you Dan?"

"I'm game, "Daniel stated and fist bumped him in agreement.

Tanya shook her head, "You two stay out of trouble!"

They stopped talking when they spotted Nell walking down the path carrying a large tray. Dean got up and went to help her.

"Thank You sir," Nell smiled at him, "When you didn't make it back for lunch I saw you were at the court. I thought you might want something to eat and drink."

"Thank you, Nell we lost track of the time," Tanya explained.

"No worries." Nell reassured them as Daniel set the tray on the table. She poured four tall glasses of lemonade with fresh strawberries floating in them. Delicious finger sandwiches sat on the crystal serving plate she set in the middle of the table.

Nancy smiled at Nell, "Thanks for thinking of us, By the way, why is the maze off limits?"

"I couldn't say miss," Nell answered shifting nervously. "Something happened a long time ago. The labyrinth has been closed since I started working here eight years ago." She gave a slight curtsy, and walked back to the hotel.

Nancy put down her lemonade and commented, "I knew something awful must have happened for them to put a fence around a perfectly good maze and lock it up."

Daniel laughed at her, "You and Tanya are the sisters of conspiracy. You could find something nefarious at a county fair."

Dean suppressed a laugh when he saw the serious look on Nancy's face. He took a finger sandwich and pointed it at her. "We'll investigate."

"Good," Nancy said.

Daniel looked over at Tanya who got up and stopped when he put up his hand and warned, "After dinner."

"That's my Daniel," Tanya replied, "Always thinking of his stomach before solving a mystery."

They heard a rustle in the honeysuckle bushes nearby. Sparky leaped over the flowerbed fence and joined them. His bushy tail wagged excitedly and he drooled when he spied the food.

Tanya broke up a chicken sandwich. She watched Sparky gobble it up hungrily and said, "I told you he always comes back for food."

After a pleasant late afternoon nap back in their rooms, the warning bell sounded. The couples woke to the dinner bell. They had 30 minutes to dress and come down to the main dining room. The brochure had informed them that it was the formal dinner of the week.

The two men wore white tuxedos and the girls wore chiffon cocktail gowns. Tanya's was turquoise and Nancy's was Mauve.

As they walked down the stairs, Nancy winked over at Tanya and whispered, "I told you we would be able to wear our bridesmaid dresses again."

"That's because Martina broke the cardinal rule of weddings and didn't make us buy ugly dresses so we wouldn't outshine the bride," Tanya replied with a laugh.

When they entered the formal dining room, four other couples were already seated at the long table. An enormous crystal Chandelier sparkled above it. The place settings were white china with gold trim. Wine glasses and water goblets were fine crystal with flower etchings. Highly polished silverware gleamed next to the plates. A gigantic ceramic tureen filled with an array of fresh flowers sat in the middle of the table flanked by two brass candelabra's

As they introduced themselves, Tanya noticed that the other guests wore styles of dress that reflected over a century of fashion. The Casey's were dressed in 1800's charm, while the Drakes, were stunning in their roaring twenties apparel. The Randolph's attire was elegant Cotton Club inspired and the Chen's wore 1950's fashion.

Nancy leaned over to Tanya, "Is this a costume ball?"

Tanya gave her a puzzled look and stated, "Mrs. Walden didn't mention it. The brochure only stated it was a formal dress affair."

The dinner was abundant and delicious. There was a large

turkey, grilled steaks, roasted asparagus and squash, buttery new potatoes, Italian salad, biscuits and apple pie with ice cream for dessert. The hearty wine that was served was Gentle Breeze Stonehouse Red.

The dinner and dancing ended well after midnight. The two couples decided to take a stroll in the gardens before they retired. When Daniel suggested walking to the maze they eagerly complied.

Curiously enough, the hedge maze was surrounded by old fashioned gas lights. Daniel gazed around to make sure no one was watching them and scaled the six foot fence, nimbly hopping over the pointed wrought iron arrows at the top.

Dean followed suit turned to the girls and said, "If we aren't back in fifteen minutes, wait fifteen more!"

Nancy laughed, "That's so old!"

Tanya looked at them through the bars and said, "Why do we have to stay behind?"

"It might not be safe," Daniel explained'

"I wasn't going to worry until you said that," Tanya replied.

The full moon broke from the puffy clouds and shone down on the girls as they waited. Five minutes later the men returned. They brushed off the leaves from their suits.

"There's another way in," Dean explained, "There's a lose bar on the right side of the fence."

"Come on," Daniel offered. Tanya looked doubtful and he asked in a taunting voice. "Don't you want to investigate?"

Nancy put her arm around Tanya and coaxed, "Come on girlfriend, where's your sense of adventure? We can't let the boys have all the fun!"

Sparky chose that moment to squeeze through the bars and exit the maze. He loped over to Tanya and sniffed her hand.

"See, Sparky wants to help." Nancy coaxed.

The group walked down the fence line until they stood before the lose rod. Daniel and Dean pulled and pulled until the bar broke lose. They couldn't remove it from the ground, so they pushed it to the side.

Dean held the bar aside while the girls squeeze through and

Daniel held it for him. Once they were all inside Daniel put the bar back in place. Two lanterns sat on the ground at the entrance of the Maze. Dean and Daniel each took a lantern and turned it on to light the way.

Sparky ran ahead of them. He paused to sniff the ground as he made each turn in the winding maze. A few times the dog moved too fast, the group lost him and had to call him back. The maze turned right and left in a dizzying fashion. The moon above them helped illuminate their progress. The dark hedges loomed on either side of them their thick leaves whispered in the breeze.

After what seemed like hours they arrived at the center of the labyrinth. A splashing lighted fountain stood on the brick patio. A life sized statue of a large buck stood in the moving water. Water poured out of his mouth into the fountain below.

The animal seemed so life-like they half expected it to leap out of the fountain and run away. Dean moved his lantern closer to read the plaque mounted on the front of the fountain wall, "In memory of King, the most evasive buck I have ever hunted." It was signed, "Jeffrey Damon III."

Nancy looked closely at the statue and said, "He sure looks like the buck I almost hit yesterday."

Dean put his arm around her and commented, "I imagine King had many offspring before he was hunted by Jeffrey."

Tanya gasped and stepped back, "Look! It moved! The statue moved!"

Nancy pointed toward the statue and cried out, "She's right! The buck's head is turned the other way!"

Daniel and Dean grinned at each other but escorted the women back into the maze. Daniel called Sparky. When the dog rushed back they moved faster. Dean stood next to Daniel and said in a whisper, "As they say in the movies, let's amscray!"

Sparky led them back through the turns of the giant puzzle. They didn't speak while they traversed the twists and turns of the hedge maze.

Finally back, they walked to the side of the fence and quickly squeezed back out through the lose bar. There was no sign of the buck, but Nancy and Tanya kept looking behind them as they walked back to the hotel. The group climbed up the stairs wished each other good night, entered their rooms and locked the doors.

Nancy was still shaking when Dean pulled her into his arms, "Hey honey, you're safe now," Dean reassured her.

"Some Nancy Drew I am," she whispered, "I know what I saw. Tanya saw it too."

Dean took her face in his hands and kissed her, "What if it's all part of the ambiance of this place, the haunted mansion, the family history and the tragic circumstances of poor Jasmine's death."

"You mean like a trick?" Nancy asked, "Then why keep the maze locked up?"

"I don't know," Dean shook his head, "Maybe some old person had a heart attack and died when they saw the statue move."

Nancy kissed Dean and said, "That would explain a lot."

Two hours later, Nancy was unable to sleep. She rose from bed sat on the window seat and gazed out over the grounds. When the moon broke through the clouds, she saw Sparky. The dog raced past the tennis courts, past the maze, and down the road to the entrance of the resort.

She decided to follow the dog to see where he went every night. She put on slacks, grabbed a t-shirt and pulled one of Dean's flannel shirts over it.

Nancy jumped when she saw Tanya in the hall grabbed at her heart and said, "Dang girlfriend, you scared the stuffing out of me!"

Tanya gasped and said, "You read my mind! I've got to know where Sparky goes!"

The two women crept down the stairs than ran lightly down the path. The moonlight led the way through the woods. Tree branches stirred and waved in the sky like reaching hands.

Up ahead they saw Sparky's tail as it whipped around the bend toward the entrance to the resort. Tanya gave a sharp cry of disappointment. The main gates had been left open and the dog raced past the entrance and onto the country road.

Nancy and Tanya had no flashlights or lanterns but the full moon gave them ample light to sprint down the road after the dog. After running about five minutes, they spotted Sparky. He sat in the middle of the road, shaking as he stared down into a ravine. The agitated dog glanced back at them and whimpered pitifully.

When the women walked up to him, he looked up at them with his tail between his legs. His large brown eyes shifted from them back to the ravine. He trotted down the hill and looked back at them a few times.

"He wants us to follow him", Tanya said.

"Okay, but be careful, the ground is bumpy," Nancy pointed out.

The women followed after him too swiftly and slipped and slid down the steep slope of the hillside. Once at the bottom, Sparky led them into the woods.

They could see lights ahead and cried out in surprise when they saw the crashed vehicle. It had rolled over after hitting a giant oak tree. The motor was still running and the front tires spun against the tree trunk.

Spunky paced nervously nearby. He looked back at the women and barked loudly. He grew more skittish as they walked toward the crash.

Mrs. Walden's words resounded in Nancy's head, "Was it a deer? That old buck causes three or four accidents every year."

Tanya pulled at her sleeve, "Nancy, we've got to see if anyone's alive!"

"You grab Sparky and keep him out of the way. I'll go check," Nancy ordered. .

Nancy moved around the vehicle, reached into the cracked window and pulled the key out of the ignition. The engine sputtered to a stop and the tires slowed their maniacal spinning. Smoke from the racing engine cleared and she peered tentatively into the smashed window.

"Nancy, is anyone alive?" Tanya asked when the tires stopped. She held onto Sparky as he squirmed and tried to get away.

Nancy's knees gave out and she sat heavily on the ground. She took a deep breath and looked over at her friend and said in a tearful voice, "No Tanya, their all dead."

Tanya walked over to Nancy. Her head was lowered and she was sobbing uncontrollably. She stepped over to the car and reluctantly looked through the windows. The moonlight gave her a clear view of the occupants. As she backed away from the car, her screams reverberated through the ravine.

Past the shards of glass she had seen them. Their broken bodies lay twisted and still like discarded ragdolls. They were all there, Daniel, Dean, Nancy, and herself. Sparky lay below her feet, crumpled and curled up into a ball.

Nancy rose to her feet and pulled Tanya away from the horrendous scene. She put her arm around her and supported her shaken form.

As they moved slowly back up the ravine she said in a gentle voice, "Let's go home, Tanya."

The two women rose slowly from the ground. Their bodies felt lighter than air. Their arms and hands were almost transparent like frosted crystal.

As they floated over the grounds past the maze they glimpsed King as he swiftly bounded over the fence of the maze. Once past the tennis courts and swimming pool, they paused and gazed up at the windows of their rooms at Gentle Breeze Resort.

"Come on Tanya, we have to hurry," Nancy pleaded, "Daniel and Dean are waiting for us."

The Hunted

The Hunted

---•---

Akara took a deep breath and scrambled up the escarpment to escape the lizard-like creature that stalked her. It snorted and breathed with a growling gurgling noise that terrified her. Adrenalin coursed through the veins of her athletic body and it answered their flight response. Her knotted leg muscles strained to put yards between herself and the predator.

Her breath was labored and she gasped as the elevation taxed her lungs. Rivulets of water dripped down her taut brown face as a light rain pelted her. The nearly sheer face of the cliff was slick with moisture and even more dangerous to scale. Akara ignored all else but the silent command of her brain. "Faster! Faster!" it urged her, "Higher! Higher!" it demanded.

She sensed the dark gray shape behind her as she struggled for each hand and foot hold. The beast clawed and snarled and pursued her with determination equal to hers. Akara had to reach the top of the mountain and the white salt flats on the plateau before the creature caught up with her.

Beyond the smooth surface of the flats were the dark cool forests, and safety. Although her mouth was dry and her lips parched, she refused to succumb to the desire to slow down and rest.

The rain continued to make the stone surface slimy and Akara slipped as she tried to find a foot hold. She lost her balance and started to fall. She threw herself against the hard stone and skidded until her right foot landed on a small ledge. She weaved precariously but righted herself and sighed with relief. Her muscles screamed for respite but she stubbornly ignored the pain. The creature that pursued her wasn't slowing down and neither would she.

As the animal closed in on her with the agility of a much smaller lizard, Akara realized she was driven by the same needs as the beast, survival. She had to escape to survive and it had to catch her to survive. It was hard to tell which emotion was the stronger. This fight for life had created a strange connection between them.

She craned her neck and calculated the distance to the top of the escarpment. The rain had stopped and the clouds finally rolled away to reveal a full moon. It glowed like a beacon and illuminated the way upward.

A myriad of stars twinkled above, like millions of eyes watching the drama below with cold detachment. On any other night she would have gazed up at them in wonder but on this night they offered little solace. Akara ignored them and concentrated on reaching the apex alive.

The creature below her appeared to slow its pace but she guessed it was a sly trick. The animal only feigned exhaustion to lull her into a sense of security. It hoped she would slow down too and be easily overtaken when it pounced.

Rather than ease her pace, Akara climbed more swiftly and evaded capture. She heard the beast grunt in frustration as it scrambled to catch up. She smiled to herself, she had judged its maneuver correctly.

"Ya!" she cried out, and climbed over the last outcropping to the top. She rolled over onto the flats and sprang to her feet. The women of her tribe were known for their speed. Akara's mother had been the fastest runner of her clan. She was the matriarch of the people.

The flats covered 2 miles of smooth, softly packed salt crystals. Akara felt on the verge of collapse but she was urged on by the knowledge that the creature would be clumsy on the squishy grainy surface. She was lighter than the beast and could sprint across the flats hardly leaving a footprint on the surface.

Beyond the flats she saw the points of light that meant she was close to her home and safety. She flew across the ghostly plain, her leather strapped feet skimming the still warm carpet. In the moonlight it looked like a field of glittering snow.

Akara glanced back and spied the dark creature in the distance. It was over 30 feet long with a long snoot and a mouth full of sharp teeth. Its head was covered with spiky formations that continued along its back to the end of a ten foot tail sporting a ball of spikes that could whip out and smash your skull like a melon. Saliva dripped from its gasping mouth as it struggled to move on the shifting terrain.

She sprinted on. Her tired legs pumped harder and harder as she strained to outlast the beast. Suddenly she tripped into one of the small sinkholes common to the flats. She relaxed her body into a ball and rolled out of the cleft, sprung to her feet and raced across the plateau.

The lights in the distance grew brighter and closer as she pushed herself even faster. She kicked up showers of salt that flew into her face and burned her eyes. Akara sputtered, spit and blew the grit from her mouth. A flood of tears washed the stinging granules from her eyes.

Burning pain seared her arms, legs and feet but sheer will power drove her onward. Quick gulps of cool night air set fire to her overtaxed lungs but she refused to relent. She was on the brink of death yet never felt more alive.

The creature behind her stubbornly slithered and skidded toward her. It had a lion's heart and continued to pick up speed. It dropped onto all fours and slid yards at a time. It then rose on all fours, bellowed loudly and leaped more yards.

Akara could respect such an animal. She understood the hunger that drove it as much as she understood her own need to escape its clutches.

As she sprinted forward towards the lights the exhausted woman thought to herself, "There can be only one winner of this race, and by the Creator, it's going to be me!"

A mere fourth of a mile now separated Akara from the boundaries of her territory. Her calves ankles and feet were in excruciating pain from lactic acid burn. She cried out and lurched forward. She was determined to reach the lights. She would be no meal for a hungry lizard.

Her eyes were riveted to the bright torches up ahead in front of the shadowed forests. She could smell the delightfully pungent odor of conifers and cried out in glee.

As Akara reached the lighted barrier, she gazed downward. The wind whipped through her waste length hair as she leaped gracefully over the eight foot ditch to safety.

She heard the beast before she saw it. It had been close at her heels. It was so consumed by the chase and its own hunger it did not see the trench until it was too late.

The surprised beast skidded helplessly near the edge, unable to stop. Its speed and massive weight carried it forward and it plunged twenty feet down into the muck and mud below.

The animal bellowed and thrashed but the more it struggled the more mired it became. After tossing and struggling for an hour, unable to get free, the animal succumbed to exhaustion and sunk. Its savage heart burst and Akara watched as it expelled its last breath with a loud sigh.

Cheers of victory erupted from the forest. It was Akara's clan members, who were eager to greet her and carve the fallen beast.

A tall, slender woman walked toward her. It was her mother. There was concern and relief in her dark eyes. She greeted her daughter with open arms and covered her shivering body with a warm animal hide.

"You did good Akara," her mother said. She was proud of her daughter, who had risked her own life to bring home food for the clan.

Life had always been this way for their clan. No one questioned the fact that someone had to drive the beast from its den in the valley below and lead it to the killing trench. Many good people had given their lives for the good of the clan. Ghostly white handprints on the walls of the caves illustrated the release of their spirits from their bodies. Sparkling crystals imbedded into the prints were the symbols of their courage and sacrifice.

Akara watched as the people carved the meat from the beast. The head would be buried in a place of honor. She felt a great sadness for the creature. The beast had been a noble adversary. She bowed her head low before the creature and praised its strength. She called out to the beast's soul, thankful for its sacrifice. Its ample flesh would feed her clan for weeks. Her people would live and thrive for another season.

To remember the clan's victory this day, the shaman of their clan would paint the cave walls with scenes of her hunt in brilliant colors, just as Akara described it. Her place in history would be documented.

Individual hand prints of the entire clan would be pressed into the mural. They would be bright crimson because on this hunt, on this day, no one lost their life.

Detour

Detour

*C*hristine made good time as she drove from St. Louis, Missouri to St. James, Missouri to visit her parents. She was just feeling relaxed about the 2 ½ hour drive when she saw a line of cars up ahead and a lighted highway sign that read, "DETOUR UP AHEAD!."

As the traffic inched forward she could clearly see what had caused the slowdown on I-44, an 18-Wheeler had jack-knifed on the rain slick pavement and blocked all but one lane.

Emergency sirens pierced the stillness of the fall morning as she followed the trail of cars and exited the highway. On impulse she followed a green Chevy pick-up truck. She assumed it would know a short cut back to the highway.

To her dismay, the driver did not lead her to the detour but instead turned off onto an old part of the highway still in use. Christine lowered her window and craned her neck and searched frantically for a street or building that looked familiar.

She passed a large road sign that looked vaguely familiar. It had a white background printed with bold black letters that read, "Missouri US 66." It was Route 66 the iconic highway she and her family had used on to travel to their annual summer vacation spots when she was a child.

The historic highway had once traversed the entire country from Springfield to Chicago and all the way to its end in California at the Santa Monica Pier.

The two-lane highway had been crowded in the summer

months with families heading out for their vacations throughout the nation. She remembered how her dad loved cruising along in their Ford Galaxy 500. They would leave at four in the morning to avoid the summer rush of tourists like themselves.

There was plenty to see without ever leaving Missouri. There were trips to Fantastic Caverns, The Crystal Cave, Branson and Silver Dollar City. They would stop at their favorite souvenir shops and eating places like Stuckey's and Dogpatch. She remembered the Wagon Wheel Cafe and the Wind Mill Restaurant.

She turned her mind back to the present and tried to drive in the direction that would take her back to I-44 but the road kept turning in the wrong direction. Frustrated and worried, Christine turned into the lot of the Route 66 Diner.

From the makes and models of the vehicles in the parking lot; old pickup trucks and mile long family station wagons, she guessed the diner had lost its tourist clientele years ago when I-44 became the main highway. She hadn't eaten breakfast and the aroma of fried bacon wafted into her open window. He stomach growled loudly. She sighed, got out of the car and thought that a nice cup of coffee would hit the spot too.

Christine sat down at a small booth and before long a waitress named "Gladys" came over to take her order. She chose scrambled eggs, bacon, toast and black coffee. The coffee came quickly and was hot and delicious.

She motioned to an elderly man at a table across from her and asked, "Excuse me sir, Can you tell me how I can get back to I-44?"

The man gave her a puzzled look, "Huh?"

Christina raised her voice thinking he was hard of hearing and explained, "I've been driving on this road for twenty minutes and must have missed the turn."

The elderly man put down his cup, looked over the top his spectacles, scratched his grizzled beard and answered, "Missy, you can't get there from here." He tipped his wrinkled cap and went back to his breakfast.

His words put Christina in an even more irritated mood. Instead of engaging the old man in further conversation, she looked around the diner for a person who might be able to give her more help.

Through the large windows of the restaurant, Christine noticed a trucker who climbed down from his cab. He walked into the diner and took a seat at the counter. He sat on a high red topped stool and ordered a gigantic breakfast. He took out a somewhat yellowed and wrinkled newspaper from his jacket, unfolded it and began to read.

Christina walked over to him and cleared her throat. When the man did not look up at her she smiled and asked in a much louder voice, "Can you help me? I got lost on this road. Can you please tell me how to get back to I-44? There was an accident on the highway and I had to take a detour and I'm afraid I'm lost."

The man looked at her with cold blue eyes and replied, "You don't have to yell girlie. I ain't deaf!" He turned back to his newspaper and said, "You can't get back to 44 from here." He chuckled and remarked, "Looks like you're in a real pickle."

Christine stared at him in disbelief. She had heard stories about how country folk felt about city folk's ways but this was the height of rudeness. She took a deep breath and persisted, "I hate to bother you again sir, but don't you have to get back on 44 to deliver your load somewhere?"

The man refused to look at her and answered in a peeved voice, "Just because I drive a truck for a living, I suppose you think I'm your personal travel guide."

Christine struggled to keep her anger out of her voice and said, "Not at all."

The man grunted and continued, "For your information little lady, this was my last stop. I just dumped my last load. Why don't you go up to the cashier and buy yourself a road map."

Christine looked at the trucker with disgust and retorted, "Well excuse me for ruining your day, but I thought truck drivers were the friendliest drivers on the road!"

At her remark several patrons turned to each other and nodded in agreement. Emboldened, Christina added, "Obviously

I've been misled by glowing TV and social media commercials about truckers."

The curious stares Christina was getting after this remark made her anxious to vacate the diner as quickly as possible. She gobbled down the rest of her breakfast, took one last gulp of her coffee, and gave the waitress a generous tip. She had visions of Gladys chasing her out into the parking lot with a formidable meat cleaver in her hand demanding a better gratuity.

She got back into her car and locked all the doors. As she headed down the road, the incident at the greasy spoon reached a nightmare quality in her mind. She shook her head and turned on the radio. A country singer belted out the words, "Don't come back!" Christine nodded her head, "No way will I come back to your little diner in this outpost of hell!"

She tuned on another channel and got a traffic report. To her great relief the accident on I- 44 had been cleared. Twenty vehicles had been involved but no one was seriously hurt.

Unfortunately the country roads kept turning the wrong way taking her further and further from the interstate. She swerved onto a gravel side road to make a U-Turn and retrace her route. She had failed to see a small "No Trespassing" sign which was blocked by overgrown weeds.

Christina started to pull out onto the main road but hesitated when she heard a popping sound. Something whizzed past her window. She quickly put the car in reverse and ended up in a muddy hole.

Another loud report had her ducking for cover. Broken glass flew everywhere as the back window of her Ford Taurus shattered. She stomped on the accelerator, braked, hit reverse and repeated this motion several times until the wheels of her car were free of the muddy rut. She maneuvered the car off the gravel and raced down the country road, without looking back.

She was easily doing 80 mph when she heard a police siren and saw flashing red lights in the rear view mirror. She repressed an angry expletive, slowed down and pulled over.

The officer who approached her car wore a brown state

trooper's hat and uniform. His mirrored sunglasses glared brightly. Christine could not see his eyes but his mouth was a thin determined line in his weathered face.

The offer's shield read, "Sgt. Randle McEvoy."

He leaned down cautiously, peered into her window and ordered, "License and registration please."

Christine gave him a nervous smile and handed him her license, registration and proof of insurance, saying, "Thank God you're here officer! I pulled over to turn around and someone shot at me! I'm sorry I was speeding but I thought someone was trying to kill me!"

Rather than expressing concern, the officer began a self-righteous tirade, "Do you know how fast you were going? This is a two-lane road. Children live in this area! I clocked you at 80 Mph! We run a quiet little town here and don't want troublemakers breaking the peace!"

"Except for the gunshots!" Christine pointed out.

"What did you say?" the officer asked coldly.

Christine answered in a clipped voice, "You run a quiet little town here, except for the gunshots fired at a woman who was lost and had to turn around on a gravel road!" Christine pointed to the back of her car, "Did you even notice that my back window is shattered and there are bullet holes all over the trunk of my car?"

"Did you even notice the "No Trespassing" sign?" The officer asked icily.

Christine glared up at him, "To be honest Sgt. McEvoy, no I did not. I was too busy trying to get the hell out of your quiet little town before I got my head blown off!"

"I'm not going to issue you a ticket," the officer stated, "In the future, ma'am please read the signs. Next time you will not get a warning. You will get a speeding ticket and a fine for driving on clearly designated private property."

As McEvoy tipped his hat and walked back to his car, she noticed he made a U-Turn in the very place where she had gotten stuck and headed in the opposite direction.

Christine pulled onto the road and speculated to herself,

"That crackpot is going to hide behind a big bush and pounce on the next unsuspecting motorist who happens to get lost in his quiet little town."

"Whatever happened to protect and serve!" she yelled out the window to no one in particular.

Christine made her way down the country road. She drove by the Route 66 Diner, slowed down and thought, "They did have delicious bacon, and eggs and the coffee was really good."

The 18-wheeler and its driver were gone from the parking lot. In fact the entire lot was empty. The diner itself looked deserted, its sign askew, its windows dirty. The pavement in the parking lot was broken in places and weeds grew up in the cracks.

Christine shook her head in puzzlement. She wondered what had happened in the last few hours that would make the diner look so vacant and the lot so desolate. The charming Route 66 Diner had become a dilapidated eyesore.

Once she passed the diner, Christine saw a sign up ahead which read, "Detour to 44 West-Next Right Turn." She cried out in relief and turned onto the detour.

As she rounded the entrance ramp to the highway she checked the rear view mirror. A metal town marker dangled at an angle from its pole and twisted in the wind.

Christine gasped at what she read. The crooked white sign with dirt smeared black letters read:

"Last Chance"

"Population: 0

"NO U-TURN!"

You Can't Go Back

You Can't Go Back

———•———

The Secretary of the Mission III Acceptance Committee looked me straight in the eyes and asked, "Miss Korvastrian, are you absolutely sure that you want to be part of Planetary Mission III?"

I returned her stare and answered, "Yes. I've thought it over quite a bit in the last 6 weeks and I want to be part of this mission."

"Unlike the other candidates," the Minister continued, "you have a loved one at home, a husband of five years, I believe?"

"My husband is in permanent cryogenic stasis," I pointed out, "Roger has a rare neurological disease and there is no cure at this time, nor will there be in the next century. He will be kept in a containment facility for the rest of his life."

The Secretary tapped her pencil on the desk and shuffled through my application.

I cleared my throat. When she looked up I pleaded, "Please don't turn me down. I need this."

The gray haired matron looked over at me, "More importantly, we need you." She noted my sigh of relief and continued, "You are one of only three in this nation who can speak the language. The colony will not survive without your expertise. Our bionic translator implants do not work efficiently on Tres Solaris."

I nodded in relief, "I'm happy to be of service."

She tapped the desk with her fingers and explained, "Normally we would not consider you an acceptable applicant but in light of your extenuating circumstances the committee has made an exception." The Secretary looked at me intently and stated, "My next question is a very important one."

I returned her gaze and she asked, "Are you willing to intermarry with one of the male inhabitants of the planet?"

I tried not to cringe at the thought. I had seen the specs. The appearance of the males that inhabited Tres Solaris was a living nightmare. I tried not to imagine such a situation and hoped no such union would be possible.

Fearful of being rejected, I reminded her of something in my file,

"You know that I'm infertile and not qualified to form a bond?"

"Yes, I did see that in the file," the Secretary agreed. She looked at me and pointed out, "It's possible that an alliance with the Tres Solarisians and the scientific community could benefit from such a union."

Now she was making me feel like a bargaining tool for politics I had no wish to participate in. I looked down at my hands and decided there was only one thing I could say, "If it comes to that, I will do it for the sake of the mission."

The woman looked relieved, brushed a strand of gray hair that had escaped her severe bun and applied a stamp of approval to my application.

With a relieved smile she stated, "You are accepted into the program. Proceed to the next room for microchip insertion."

"Thank You," I replied gratefully.

As I rose from my chair, the Secretary grabbed my arm and said, "Remember, you can't go back."

I gently brushed her hand from my arm and answered confidently, "Yes, I understand."

"Good," she replied. Pulling out the folder for her next applicant she added, "Good luck and as they say, Godspeed!"

I walked down to the end of a long gray hallway were I saw a sign which directed me with the words, "Applicant Receiving Area." A black arrow pointed to the right and I entered a large conference room where I joined a long line behind a plethora of other young women.

As I surveyed the crowd, I thought to myself how eager we were, so willing to be good little guinea pigs for this grand experiment that had failed two previous times. I wondered if the others were as desperate as I was to get off this dying planet.

As I scanned the large room filled with desks and medical staff in lab coats, the lack of males among the population disconcerted me. I am suspicious by nature and tried to tell myself that the males were being processed in another conference room, or another facility.

Ahead of me, a very young woman sniffed quietly as crocodile tears streamed silently down her soft cheeks.

Feeling a stab of compassion, I gently touched her sleeve and asked, "Are you all right?"

The petite young woman turned around and looked up at me. Her large violet eyes were misty with tears. She nodded and replied, "I guess I'm being childish but they cut off most of my hair! I've never had it cut before."

Many young women in our nation had continued the tradition of not cutting their tresses since they were born. I had trimmed my hair years earlier when Roger had entered the life support facility. I could sympathize with her. I nearly wept when my long brown tresses had fallen to the floor.

She had the most beautiful reddish brown hair with golden highlights. It was shoulder length but still lovely as it billowed around her heart-shaped face.

"I know how difficult that must have been," I consoled her, "but I'm sure you realize that for travel and sanitary purposes it was necessary."

She nodded, "I have to go on this mission. I am classified as infertile. My parents are dead and I have no relatives left." She let me absorb that information and continued with a tone full of pride, "They need me. After all, I'm a registered Healer."

A Healer was a woman born with an uncanny ability to heal the sick by placing her hands on them. She would say prayers, go into a meditative state and detect the medical problems inside a person.

I smiled and said, "I'm impressed. I've never met a Healer."

This wasn't quite true. I had met one when Roger had fallen ill. The ancient Healer had placed her arthritic hands on him and nearly collapsed. She had shaken her head with tears in her eyes and had told me that Roger would never recover in this life.

I decided not to burst her bubble of pride and commented, "I'm thankful we are traveling together. It's quite possible we will survive this trip because you will be on board."

"Thank You," she looked at me shyly, "My name is Rena. I hope we can be friends."

"I'm Sathra," I replied with a smile, "I would be honored to be your friend, "I'm a linguist. I speak and translate Tres Solarisian."

Rena smiled and commented, "You are as rare a breed as I."

"You see," I nodded in agreement, "we already have something in common, we are crucial to the success of this mission."

"And ever so modest," Rena returned with a slight smile

I grinned back, "We have a lot of influence here, let's request that we become a team."

"Could we?" Rena asked, "I would like that. Together we can unify and save our two cultures."

"Provided the Tres Solarisians feel they need saving," I agreed.

"We have to fix things so we don't have to be a part of the assimilation though," Rena pointed out. Her eyes narrowed, "You know what it means. We would have to fraternize with the males."

"I certainly hope not!" I exclaimed. "I was willing to help with communications and translations as a professional colleague but not that."

The line moved forward more quickly and Rena and I waved to each other as we continued to separate tables for our physicals. She and I prepared for our Monitor Chip insertions. Once we passed the initial physical we moved on to surgery.

My technician, a statuesque woman in a white lab coat, goggles and a mask, smeared a topical solution on the back of my neck right below the hairline to freeze the area. I felt a slight pressure as she made a tiny incision into my skin and the chip was inserted. The incision was sealed and the chip was downloaded to the system. Mission Control could now track my every movement on the ship and later on Tres Solaris from the M.S.S.S. (Midway Stealth Space Station).

Rena, I and a group of 24 other women were ushered to the Mission Medical Facility to receive inoculations that would protect us from microbes and diseases indigenous to our destination planet.

The Colony Mission scientists had studied the data on Missions I & II. Mission I had failed almost immediately. A team of 20 Travelers had made contact with city dwellers. They were misunderstood as invaders and killed within minutes. Scientists concurred that a large landing party could be considered a threat.

Mission II was another disaster. The team landed in the center of a Tres Solarisian military base which was mistakenly thought to be a research center. Before their chips were removed, vital medical, technological and societal information had been downloaded. After a few days, the team's chips went silent and no further communications were received.

Because of those catastrophic failures, it became imperative to attempt colonization without being discovered. The first gen microchips had not worked consistently and technologists had assumed magnetic waves, sunspots and atmospheric anomalies could have scrambled their reception.

The chip malfunction had been corrected by coating it with a layer of Chronium II, a lab created alloy that was resistant to magnetic disruptions.

I looked over at the other women as they stood in huddled groups and realized we all had one thing in common, each of us had our own unique reasons for going on an obviously dangerous mission. We no longer feared the unknown. Apparently, we all had decided it couldn't be worse than what we left behind.

Every participant was a young, highly intelligent, perfect physical specimen. Most of the women were fertile and possessed a unique survival skill. They were experts as engineers, research scientists, medical personnel, technologists, teachers and care givers.

Once on the Mother Ship, candidates would be indoctrinated

in language, and customs. After intensive survival training we would be placed in our cryogenic tubes for our deep space journey of 5 years. At the end of our sleep, the Auto-Tron Navigator would awaken us two weeks before planet drop.

Unlike previous missions, our teams would be dropped by night into Safe Zones; areas of sparse population. Assimilation would be a gradual process. We would spend many months in our bio domes undergoing the biological and environmental adaptations necessary to survive on our new home

Rena and I continued our six weeks of rigorous pre-flight training. It was the same training all astronauts endured. We were tested with all kinds of deprivations; food, sleep, contact, sight and sound.

I worked with the Language Supervisor and taught basic Tres Solarisian dialects. After class, I tutored Rena more extensively. By the time we were ready to file into the Mother Ship, she had become quite fluent.

During our training weeks, I had learned that Rena was ten years younger than me. I became to think of myself as a big sister to her. Our friendship became more solid in those weeks.

Unfortunately, Rena and I had become pariahs to the other women. They were wary of us and remained at arm's length even in group activities. When we ate meals we sat alone. The women whispered to each other and gazed over at us with undisguised suspicion. Rena had suggested it was because of our unique skills, while I suspected it was because our infertility.

A big part of the other women's acceptance into the program was because they were willing to make babies and create hybrids with Tres Solarisians. They were taught to believe they were the last hope of our dying race. Because they were perfect female specimens they received special hormone injections so they would appeal to the males of Tres Solaris.

As I waited for the order to enter the sleep tube, I considered how many centuries it had taken for women to earn equal rights on our own planet. In spite of our struggles, it seemed that females were still only valued for their biological ability to conceive and give birth.

The people of our home planet were painfully aware of why this space mission was necessary. Our once pristine world was slowly dying. We had nearly exhausted our natural resources and global warming resulted in massive weather changes. Floods, droughts, electrical storms, earthquakes, hurricanes had increased much earlier than predicted.

I recalled that one eminent scientist, Dr. Mahotra, had called our century the "Third Extinction Era." Four of the smaller continents were nearly under water. Half of the population of our world had perished because of a raging pandemic that lasted nearly five years. Synthetic food was manufactured and had all but replaced agricultural products. Nearly all of the rain forests had been replaced by human habitation. Flooding covered 1/3 of the planet when glaciers and icecaps had melted by 40%. The populations of plants and trees were nearly decimated. Oxygen levels diminished with each passing year.

We had no choice but to move out into space. Ten colonies had been established on the moon, but water and air had to be recycled. Every nation was asked to sacrifice food and resources to keep what politicians called "The New Earth Experiment" alive. After 15 years the experiment failed and the survivors returned home.

A decade later a new planet was discovered by an amateur scientist, James Tres and a Nobel Prize winning astronomer, Anna Solaris, hence the name Tres Solaris. The governments of the world began to call it our future home.

Five years later an unmanned probe was sent to Tres Solaris. The photos "Mini RoBo" sent back had been promising. They had revealed a world with an oxygen rich atmosphere similar and far less polluted than ours. Its oceans and continents were teeming with plant and animal life. There was only one problem; intelligent beings already populated the planet.

Pragmatists had urged world governments to continue with "assimilation" while the moral minority had coined their plan "a mass invasion". Thousands of conscience ridden citizens protested and marched to the seats of their governments with signs reading, "Hell no, we won't go!" and, "Are We the Alien Invaders?"

When massive earthquakes had rocked the continents killed millions and destroyed ocean-side communities and mountain cities, the moralist's voices had been drowned out by those who wanted to survive.

A compromise had been reached to insure that moving to another planet would be feasible and morally correct. Peaceful missions would be sent, manned by ambassador astronauts that would infiltrate the indigenous population and make contact with amenable scientists who would support our plan.

The idea was sound but had become a disaster. The ambassador astronauts of mission I had been annihilated because there had been no consistent way to observe the planet until Dr. Zanthros, Head of Planetary Missions had suggested that a series of probes be sent that listened and stored Tres Solarisian data. Later, renowned linguists had created a language program that could be downloaded and stored.

I had enrolled in the Alien Languages program after getting my Bachelor degree in college. I also earned a Master's Degree in Psychology and the first Bachelor's Degree in Alien Civilization.

My professors quickly realized I had a knack for languages. They discovered I could not only read and write in Tres Solarisian but I could mimic the accents, sounds and inflections like a native. They had conferred with me and recommended me to the National Space Association and Mission III. I had agreed wholeheartedly. I had been eager to embark on a journey to a new land.

The five years in cryo-sleep went quickly. As I became wakeful, I remembered a dream about Tres Solaris. In my dream, I was swathed in some kind of filmy membrane. I had clawed my way out of the sticky shroud and the filmy material had torn away piece by piece. I had made an opening large enough to release my head, had gasped for air and had squeezed the rest of my exhausted body free.

Fortunately the cryo-chamber had recognized the dream was

too intense and had increased endorphin levels in my brain to insure my continued sleep. However, the medication had failed to prevent the scary residual memory of the nightmare when I woke up.

I remained prone while the bio tech robot removed the tubes and chemical patches that had given me life support for five years.

Electrical impulses had stimulated my muscles to prevent atrophy but as I stood up, I felt weak. I was groggy and dizzy and didn't feel comfortable in my own skin. I had been warned of the side effects of deep sleep during my training. I was told that Tres Solarisian nutrients would be put in my body to give me my "planet-legs" as they called it.

We had all been instructed that DNA changes would be necessary to adjust to our new environment. We had to adapt to an alien ecosystem which did have many similarities to our home planet.

I and all the other women had signed the disclaimer concerning risk of death and other side effects. We all understood that were part of a celestial ark and two by two we would be deposited on an alien world to unite two civilizations birthed by the stars.

Next to me, Rena stirred, sat up in her sleep chamber and looked around. There was confusion in her violet eyes until she saw me. A weak smile curved her lips and lit up her ashen cheeks.

I walked over and took her arm as she climbed from the tube. After she became steady on her feet, we joined the line of twenty four other women who had disembarked from their tiny domiciles.

Once again we were checked over by physicians. After we were given a good report, we filed into the mess hall for our first real meal in five years. It was a meager disappointing affair of liquid proteins and water. The nutritionist informed us more solid foods would be gradually introduced as the week went on. The closest thing we got to chew on was a cherry flavored gelatin mixture which contained mega doses of Vitamin D, iron and calcium to replace the nutrients that had been depleted during our deep space flight.

I enjoyed getting reacquainted with Rena the next two weeks as we prepared for planet drop. We trained daily to get our muscles back in shape, viewed videos of Tres Solaris and practiced our language skills.

We learned that Tres Solaris was sparsely populated with intelligent beings that lived in carefully monitored highly social communities. Their laws were similar to our Ten Precepts.

I was a bit skeptical of about that discovery. Throughout our planet's history some of the most brutal and aggressive policies were doled out in the name of our Ten Precepts. Like the fertility clause of the last decade. Women like Rena and I were discriminated against because we could not add to the embryo storage facility in our state.

I discussed this issue with Rena at our evening meal, "What we have here is a hypocritical doctrine we are asked to carry to a new world."

"I guess we really won't know what to expect until we live there," Rena pointed out.

"I suppose they are trying to make our mission as positive as possible," I agreed, "They don't want us to change our minds at the last minute."

Rena chuckled softly, "It would be terrible if the most important mission to save our people dissolved into mutiny and anarchy."

"You many laugh," I commented, "but when we had to look at those anatomical diagrams of Tres Solarisians, the thought of jumping ship did cross my mind but for the fact we are orbiting in deep space."

Rena's smile faded, "Sathra, do you think we are going to our certain death?"

"Let's just say that we are certainly going to enter a different life, "I answered, hoping to soothe her worries.

We would disembark from the mother ship in pairs and be jettisoned onto the planet's surface in the dead of night. Our locations were plotted for exact targets.

Rena and I would be placed in a forest area in the center of one of the continents in the northern hemisphere. We would be provided with a detailed map of the nearest towns and cities that was downloaded onto our mobile tracking device. Once on Tres Solaris we would have a quarantine time in our Bio Dome habitat for six months. It would take time for our bodies to adjust to the climate and atmosphere.

What no one mentioned is that some of us would probably not survive the drop and others would not survive the confinement. From what I had read about the last two missions a 20% attrition rate could be expected. Dr. Narov, our training physician, informed Rena and I that under the new plan attrition would 1% or less. He assured us that we had a 99.9% probability of survival not only because of our unique skills but our adaptation to the pre-drop biological additives was above average.

He told us that our team was his biggest hope for success. He explained that while the other women were sent to procreate and continue our race with the Tres Solarisians, our role was to prepare the way for future missions.

When the day arrived for planet drop we were allowed to choose our favorite foods for our last meal. Rena and I looked at each other as we dined on fresh fruits and vegetables. I sighed then whispered, "Like the last meal of the condemned!"

Rena nodded and added, "Or lambs to the slaughter."

I sipped my herbal tea and said, "Rena, can we make a pact right now, before we go down there?"

"Yes, absolutely," she replied with a smile.

My hand trembled as I reached for hers, "Let's make a pact to survive no matter what it takes."

She took my hand and replied, "I promise we will survive no matter what!"

I smiled back at her and added, "Rules be damned, mission be damned, we will find a way to live on Tres Solaris because we have no choice."

Rena's left eyebrow raised, "My sentiments exactly!"

I took a breath and asked, "Friends forever no matter what?"

"That's a promise," Rena complied.

Our pod was ready its engines nearly silent as we stowed our supplies and pulled on our suits and helmets. Our vehicle was a shiny ebony titanium material with a magnetic shield which rendered it invisible to the human eye and undetectable on radar. It would jettison us into the atmosphere and at five hundred feet shoot out black parachutes like a bloated porcupine and gently land.

We belted ourselves into the pod, closed our helmets and turned on our communications. We had slept for five years and trained for this moment for nearly six months.

The monitors displayed our heartbeats as they beat wildly in anticipation. There was a whoosh of air and our pod burst out of the mother ship like a cannon ball. After we orbited around Tres Solaris twice, our autopilot ignited the cold fusion engine and shot us into the planet's atmosphere.

I looked out the tiny windows one last time before the shutters closed to protect us from the heat and atmospheric radiation of entry. The full moon overhead reflected a dark purple night sky brightening into violet, the color of Rena's eyes. The continents below were darkest green. Fluffy white clouds drifted above the continents. A rosy sunset splashed ebony mountain ridges. Dark forests interspersed with silver meandering rivers gave way to urban areas illuminated with sparkling city lights.

When we were about a thousand feet above the continent, the pod rolled and rotated slowly into a landing trajectory. Wisps of air burst from hundreds of orifices on the hull to slow us down. The foliage below approached rapidly. At 500 feet the pod slowed down. At two hundred feet the parachutes deployed and we swerved away from tall trees and rocky bluffs. The winds and rotations carried us to our landing site, an open meadow covered with waves of dark grasses.

We landed with a slight thump and rolled a few hundred feet. The parachute bubbles deflated and the landing tripod was released from its hangar. I looked over at Rena and we smiled at each other.

"We made it," I said with a sigh of relief.

"100% in this pod survived the drop!" Rena exclaimed.

Both of us scrambled from our seats and grabbed our survival packs. We pressed the button and opened the hatch, but we were reluctant to remove our helmets until our bio scanners informed us that the air was safe to breathe.

We gripped hands and lowered ourselves onto the ground. Rena walked ahead and turned around to survey the moonlit terrain. I looked up at the heavens and surveyed an immense canvas of stars in the night sky.

I bowed my head and summoned the protection of the Creator who had made this world and all that was in it. Rena stood by my side, bowed and whispered her own prayers.

The storage hatch on the landing pod contained a Mobile Auto-Tron unit which carried supplies for our adaptation period. I ejected it from the hold and pressed the activation button.

The metal container opened and our Personal Auto-Tron detached itself and moved toward us. Its head and body were composed of a shiny alloy but the face was covered with an artificial material which gave it an odd appearance. Braids of coiled metal sprang from its head and its eyes were large and silvery with prismatic irises. Blackish eyebrows arched sharply as the robot's head swiveled to look at us. The Auto-Tron rose from its bent position and stood upright. Its body was about 4 feet tall, a shiny copper color and had the appearance and proportions of a female. It wore a dark brown work suit and thick black boots.

The Auto-Tron rolled toward us, cocked its metallic head, smiled with thin buff colored lips and said, "Hello, I am MAGN, your Mobile Automated Ground Navigator.

Rena and I stared at the unit and said hello in unison.

"You may call me Mag," it continued. "You may think of me as the matriarch of your family." The robot froze and her braids vibrated. She continued with, "I have scanned the atmosphere and it is safe for you to breath now."

Rena and I smiled at each other and removed our helmets. We took a deep breath and shook out our sweaty hair in relief. A cool breeze stirred around us which was a welcome relief from the cooped up confines of space travel

"Come," Mag announced in her pleasant voice, "I will guide you to a safe location and help you erect your bio-dome."

Mag rolled to the ship and unloaded a cart with a huge eight by ten box on its bed. She uploaded herself to the front as wheels lowered from her boots. She pulled the cart and moved along the terrain towards the tree line.

I looked over at Rena and commented, "Mag is certainly unusual."

"For sure!" Rena agreed, "most Auto-Trons are silver and lack expression."

It was sunset on Tres Solaris when Mag led us into a forest of tall stately trees. As Mag pulled the cart through the woods, her metallic braids bobbed up and down. Night creatures and insects called to each other as we traversed the area.

I sprinted ahead and jogged next to the Auto-Tron and asked, "Mag are those metallic tendrils like hair?"

"I require no hair," Mag answered looking straight ahead, "The tendrils you are referring to are microbe and air sample collectors to monitor the atmosphere for your safety and scientific analysis."

Rena jogged forward turned to Mag and asked, "Mag will you be with us for the duration?"

"I have a lifespan of over 100 years with my self-maintenance program. I will be your guide and protector on this lifelong mission. It is my number one priority."

This seemed to comfort Rena as we trudged through a thick undergrowth of vines and bushes which were mercifully flattened down by the heavy cart.

Mag paused and turned her shoulder pads into spotlight mode, illuminating the surrounding woods. She moved her head to the right and left as her eyes assessed the trail. She stopped near an outcropping of tall rocks whose smooth surface formed a natural retaining wall and announced, "The Bio Dome will go here."

We removed our packs and with Mag's go ahead we took off our containment suits. Dressed in our dark blue jumpsuits and boots, we helped clear the perimeter of smaller rocks and debris.

After clearing a 20 X 20 foot area, we watched as Mag unloaded the large storage crate from the cart. It weighed hundreds of pounds but she lifted it like it was a cardboard box.

Our Bio-Dome was a large oval shape when it was erected. Its outer skin was tough and made from a rubbery artificial material that could withstand heat, cold, floods, earthquake, high winds or even explosives. Its mirrored surface reflected the surroundings and rendered it invisible from the outside yet we could survey the environment from the inside.

Inside the lower cabinet of the storage cart were several smaller crates loaded with furniture. Mag unfolded the supply cabinets and set them up against the far wall. Rena and I put together our sleeping cots and bed side tables. A folding screen was available to place in between the beds if we needed more privacy. We set that aside next to the storage cabinets.

Mag busied herself setting up our portable food processor and refrigeration units. There was an air cooler and circulator which doubled as a heating unit in the winter season.

Extra air tanks were available to recycle and cleanse the air because the outside atmosphere would be filtered for safety. If Mag or the portable air analyzer assessed an outside contagion was present the dome would seal itself and provide us with pure uncontaminated air until the microbes were studied and a treatments completed.

We would continue to breathe the air of Tres Solaris as we had been trained. With the help of continued exams and bio modifications we would adapt to the microbes that naturally occurred. Our bodies would produce antibodies and defense mechanisms to fight against indigenous diseases. It was essential that we build up a healthy immune system for survival on this planet.

Mag moved around the room and briskly completed her tasks. She set up a kitchen station, a study station, medivac unit, a shower and latrine. As Mag zipped around the room I realized she looked more like a Tres Solarisian than one of us.

I mentioned this to Rena. She nodded and pointed out, "This was probably planned to help us get used to their appearance."

"True," I agreed, "Theoretically with a gradual exposure we should adjust. Mag however is more beautiful than them in her own way."

"See it worked," Rena stated, "She no longer seems so odd and ugly after today."

Our mandatory quarantine would last 2 months. Mag replaced our nutrient patches with injections of stronger doses. We practiced our language skills each day and did not venture out into the open.

Rena and I alternated from moving about to semi-conscious states or comatose states in our sleeping cots. Mag was our doctor and nurse on constant duty with the medivac unit.

Our microchips were downloaded with educational information so we could assimilate; detailed knowledge of the planet and people of Tres-Solaris. At the same time information about our experiences was sent back to the Mother ship.

Once our quarantine period ended, Rena and I took short trips outside to study the climate and terrain around our habitat. Our bodies had changed so that the world did not seem alien but more familiar. We delighted in every tree, sniffed every blossom and pointed out every avian creature to each other. To our delight, small woodland creatures appeared and approached us without fear.

Mag led us to a slivery stream a few miles from our camp, and we stuck our naked toes in the water and giggled like children at how cold it was. A tiny flying insect alit on Rena's hair. She was afraid to move and hurt it, so I blew at it gently and it flitted away.

The gravity on Tres Solaris was less than our home planet and the air more oxygenated. We could trek for miles without getting tired. With Mag's help we harvested edible plants and fungi to add to our evening meals. Fruits and berries were picked, analyzed by Mag and sampled by us.

We did not kill any wildlife. Rena and I had taken a similar vow never to eat the flesh of another living creature.

After weeks of trekking through the forests and traversing the meadows and hilly regions of our new home, we noticed that in spite of wearing patches against harmful UV rays, the sun had turned our skin to a tawny brown color. The hair on our arms and legs had thinned and turned wispy and golden.

The many changes we underwent the next months were gradual and each one was assimilated and became the norm. One evening Mag told us it was time for our final phase of adaptation.

We were confined to our beds and put under anesthesia. Mag would instigate and monitor our final assimilation procedure. Days went by as we slept. During periods of wakefulness, I reached for Rena's hand and she took mine. Mag became a shiny blur as she gazed down at us with her kaleidoscope eyes. She turned her thin lips up into a thin reassuring smile as we faded into oblivion once again.

At the beginning of our sixth month on Tres Solaris, I stirred and became aware of my surroundings. Mag removed tubes and IV lines from my arms. She gently removed the bandages which had encased my entire body.

It was early morning and the habitat was lit only by the faint glow of the monitors on the medivac units. As I rose to a sitting position I felt instantly dizzy. My eyes felt strange and watered incessantly. The rest of my body felt odd, as if I had lost a lot of weight. As I swung my legs over the side of my cot, it felt as if my skin had tightened over my bones.

As I stepped down onto the floor, I could barely see my own legs and feet. My limbs were too light and smooth and felt like hollow sticks. I touched my arm and nearly cried out. Only the tiniest and thinnest of hair covered my wiry muscles. I raised my hand. My entire hand was bare and my long fingers stuck out like bony spikes. The nails were short, stubby and ugly.

My flat board-like feet sported five stubby toes with flat nails devoid of the beauty I had been so proud of.

I staggered over to Rena's bed and drew back with a fearful cry. She was gone! A horrible alien creature was lying in her place.

Mag grabbed my arms as I ran past the sleeping cots and headed for the door. In panic mode, I tried to push her away. I was terrified the thing on the bed would come after me.

Mag held onto me with a vice-like grip and said, "Don't be afraid. Look at her eyes."

Mag steered me back toward the cot. I cringed, gritted my teeth and ventured a swift glance at the hideous creature on Rena's bed.

Imbedded in the flat face with a small chopped off nose and a tiny slit of a mouth were two large violet eyes. My heart sank. The thing on the bed was no monster, it was Rena.

I scurried outside too look at my own reflection on the surface of our habitat. I put my boney fist in my slack mouth, bit down with dull filed down teeth and suppressed a shrill cry of horror. I too had been transformed.

I recalled the question of the matron at the Mission Acceptance office, "Are you absolutely sure that you want to be a part of Planetary Mission III?"

Had I not been so irritated, I might have heard a warning plea in her voice. Words she uttered before I went in for my physical came back to haunt me the most. She had grabbed my arm and said, "You can't go back!"

I slumped to the ground and wept. I cried out in rage, "So this was their great plan, to turn us into them?" I began to laugh a hysterical laughter which quickly transformed into a high-pitched keening.

Mag stood next to me in a quandary as to what to do. I wiped my face and rose slowly as Rena walked shakily towards us. Tears streamed from her still beautiful eyes onto her bony alien face.

She clutched at the wiry dull strands of her very short hair, fell on her knees and exclaimed, "Sathra why have they done this to us!"

I knelt next to her and put my arm around her, "I think we have been assimilated."

Mag looked down at both of us and produced a syringe, "You must take this. It will help you adjust to your new form."

As the medicine hit my bloodstream a sense of calm came over me. I looked up at Mag, "I want more of that."

Mag injected Rena, looked over at me and said, "In six hours you will get another dose."

I helped Rena to her feet. As we held onto each other and walked back to the habitat, Mag whirred by our side.

I turned to the Auto-Tron and asked, "What is the name of this planet?"

Mag cocked her head and answered, "Tres Solaris."

"I know that," I stated, "What do Tres Solarisians call this planet?"

Mag's eyes twirled like prisms as she replied, "Earth. It is called Earth."

I sat down on my cot, "Well I guess we are now officially "Earthlings." I looked down at my strange hands, "we are not the alien invaders we were supposed to be after all."

Rena sat down next to me and touched my arm, "But we are still us. In our cells and DNA there is still a lot that is us. In our minds and hearts, you are Sathra and I am Rena."

I gave her a weak smile, "Let's make a pact to survive no matter what."

"Done," Rena answered and gripped my hand tightly.

I squeezed her hand, "Friends forever?"

Her answer was quick and firm, "Friends forever, no matter what!"

I smiled at Rena and in my mind I hatched a plan. First of all, I had to figure out how to get these cursed monitor chips out of our necks. Next, I had to get Mag to join us, or find a way to shut her off!

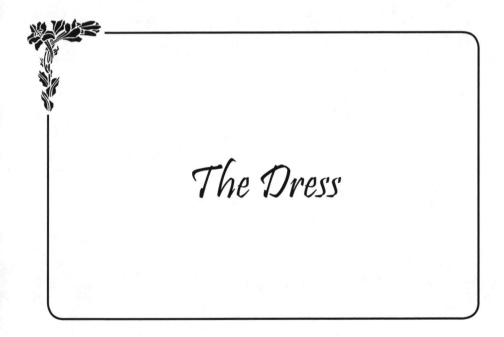

The Dress

The Dress

Catherine Chapman, the daughter of Victor Chapman I, Candles Resort magnate, scoured the fashion magazines for the perfect dress. Not any designer dress would do, this one had to be an original, like her. She was convinced that Gerald Abernathy Tiergarten II would propose to her this Friday at Tony's Restaurant.

"What a catch he is, "she thought, "and so lucky to have me!"

Cat, as her friends called her, surveyed her perfect figure for the third time in the triple mirror of the dressing room at Nichole's Dress Shop on 10th Street in downtown St. Louis.

She was very pleased at her appearance. "I've come a long way," she told herself, "that gawky teen with braces and funky glasses of five years ago is gone." She couldn't remember why she had fought with her mother about trips to the orthodontist, not to mention how she had hated the skin treatments at the Diamond Spa.

Father had presented her with the ultimate gift, plastic surgery to correct a slight bump on the ridge of her nose. Rhinoplasty had been excruciatingly painful after the anesthetic had worn off. She had sported an unlovely swollen nose and black eyes for several months. She nearly missed a whole summer season at the Lake of the Ozarks.

She had given father such a hard time. She had balked and complained that having her nose fixed would erase her authentic self. When she had seen the final result, she quickly put away her unrealistic ideals. After all, the payoff had been a perfect face for her senior year of high school.

When she turned 21 her parents had agreed to breast enhancement, and some carefully done body sculpting. That spring she was photographed in a stunning thousand dollar designer bikini on the beach at Candles Resort. To her surprise the photograph was highlighted in the Ladue News.

She had earned a Communications degree from Washington University and specialized in Media. The next five years she worked in Public Relations for her father's Resorts in Branson and at the Lake of the Ozarks.

The local tabloids and social media had documented her every move. They often referred to her as the Princess of the Midwest.

That summer she had met and been wooed by the man of her dreams, whose father was the 10th richest man in the world. Gerald Abernathy Tiergarten II was the tall, ruggedly handsome, and Harvard educated vice-president of his father's software company, located in Clayton Missouri.

Cat stepped over the expensive garments she had rejected and dropped to the dressing room floor. She turned to the couturier's owner with a frown and whined, "Nothing will do, Nichole. I had hoped I would find something magical here, that heads would turn when I entered the room."

"Madame could turn heads in a gunny sack," Nicole flattered.

Cat pointed to the layers of discarded dresses on the floor, "If these turned heads they would surely lament, "last year's designs." I saw many of them at the Paris spring preview 'last year'."

Fearful of losing her best client, Nichole suggested, "There is a dress that just came in, dear Cat. I believe its designer will challenge all others this year, Omri Sanathra, a lovely woman from India. Her creations can only be described as spun cream and soft clouds."

Cat's green eyes widened, she tossed her shiny auburn hair, "Let me see it. You owe me the first look, considering the thousands of dollars I have spent in your shop this year alone."

"Cherie, you are a friend," Nichole reassured her, "Of course you will be the first. When I saw the lovely creation, I immediately thought of you. I will even let you take it home and try it out."

Cat grinned, her face flushed with the excitement that a new expensive treasure always gave her.

Back at her Penthouse apartment near the St. Louis Arch, Cat removed the new dress from its pink flowered box, carefully moving aside the delicate white tissue paper that enshrouded it.

The icy blue cocktail dress was light as a feather. She ran her soft manicured fingers over the breathtaking material. It felt like the soft petals of a delicate rose. Cat carefully slipped it over her head. The material glided down her body like silk. It settled prettily, softly skimming lightly over her curves.

The neckline was gently scalloped, dipped slightly over her breasts and displayed enough cleavage to be sensual but not vulgar. The tiny capped sleeves dropped lightly over her narrow shoulders. The dress was fitted at the waste, clung slightly to her slender hips and the skirt flowed softly to four inches above her knees.

Cat studied her image in the mirror. After a few minutes she felt dizzy, closed her eyes and leaned on her boudoir chair. Her stomach lurched and she sat down.

When she opened her eyes, she no longer saw her own image in the mirror. A disturbing scene enfolded before her eyes. Some quirk of fate had shown a vision of a day in the life of a young Indian woman. Like a video, she watched moments of another person's life.

The young woman sat at a long table bent over a sewing machine. She was doing piece work in a suffocating factory with at least one hundred other Indian women. The girl lifted her head and wiped away her sweat with a cloth. Cat immediately recognized her was the younger version of Omri Sanathra the designer of the dress she wore.

The Omri in her mirror was not much past being a teenager. The young woman was extremely thin with thick black tresses pulled back into a braid. Her velvety brown skin was flawless and wet with sweat that dripped down her long neck and seeped through her blue flowered shift. Her face was lean and beautiful, and her large dark oval eyes with dark shadows beneath were riveted to the sewing job in front of her. Nimble fingers swiftly moved the fabric through the machine. Her apparent fatigue spoke of back breaking work and sleepless nights.

A plaintive sound erupted from a cloth covered basket next to her on the sewing table. Cat leaned forward and peered closer to see what was in the basket. A tiny baby boy with a full head of ebony hair and pudgy little balled fists stirred from his nap. He looked up at his mother and gurgled. Omri cooed at him softly gently rocking the basket until he fell back to sleep.

"Sleep well, David," the young mother whispered, "It will be all right sweet boy. It is for you that I work so hard and for your papa to make ends meet while he goes to University."

An unusual feeling pierced Cat's heart. She watched with empathy as the young woman worked frantically into the night to complete as many pieces as she could until a bell sounded and it was quitting time.

Cat intercepted Omri's thoughts as she picked up baby David and prepared to leave. Omri's husband, Sanje was in medical school. He worked 16 hours a day as an intern in a busy hospital in New Delhi. The young family lived in a tiny two room bungalow with Sanje's widowed mother.

Rathna, Omri's mother-in-law, took in laundry and ironing for wealthy clients. It was back breaking work and earned little money but she insisted she do her part.

Rathna was a little hard on her daughter-in-law, who was ten years younger than her son. The saving grace to Omri was that she doted on her grandson and watched him during the day. She even brought David to her work place so Omri could breast feed and cuddle with him.

Cate started to sweat as she felt the oppressive heat from the factory. She could hardly breathe for the stale air in that dimly lit room. She found it difficult to fathom how Omri could remain so sweet, so positive considering the abject misery of her situation.

When she came to her senses the socialite shook her head. Her reflection stared back at her from the mirror. At first she dismissed the incident as a fever dream brought on by anxiety and an empty stomach. She carefully removed the lovely dress, placed it on its silk-covered hanger and hung it in her walk-in closet.

Cat sponged off her face and body, touched up her makeup and brushed her hair into place. She was meeting her best friend Liv for lunch at Chez Paris in twenty five minutes.

She wore a lovely gray swing jacket with a thinly pleated skirt paired with a pale pink silk blouse. Her Prada shoes and purse were rosy pink. At the last moment she swished on a gorgeous filmy scarf splashed with pink and gray swirls.

Even the designer suit could not still the somber feelings that remained from the vision in the mirror. Cate greeted Liv with an air kiss as she joined her at their favorite table near the multi-paned windows of Chez Paris.

"What's going on girlfriend," Liv asked as they toasted with wine glasses.

Cat relayed her curious experience to her friend. Not wanting to spook her, she described it as a dream rather than a vision.

Liv cocked her head, pushed an errant dark brown curl from her forehead and stared at her with wide hazel eyes and said, "What a terrible dream! Don't dare give it another thought. Everyone knows about the conditions in those factories. It's up to their government to make improvements. I'm sure it has improved in the last ten years with the increased modernization going on in India. The dress sounds divine. Let's plan on seeing Omri's complete line this spring."

"You don't understand, Liv," Cat frowned, "I feel badly for the poor woman. What she had to go through in her young life is appalling."

Liv shrugged her shoulders and glanced at the menu, "Cheer up girl. Let's order lunch. The shrimp salad looks good."

"I want to learn more about Omri," Cat insisted.

Olive took a sip of her wine, "The best thing you can do is wear her designs and make her famous. How she lived doesn't matter. What matters is that wearing that dress you will charm Gerald into finally asking you to marry him."

After lunch Cat returned to her apartment still troubled by

her vision. She had not realized before that her conversations with Liv were always so superficial. She changed the subject when Cat brought up anything serious. She would nod or shrug and revert to shallow speak. Things like, where would her next vacation with Gerald be spent, or where he was taking her to dinner, or if they had found a suitable home yet.

Cat remembered that in high school she would always ask questions during her lessons. She had wanted to know the truth about others and herself. She had always felt that the world could be a better place if people would just have empathy and walk in another person's shoes.

Cat remembered a lively discussion in American History class at Washington University. The class was studying the Civil Rights and the Woman's Rights Movement of the 60's. In World History class, she had studied the social climate in India and how women still struggled to be heard.

She was wealthy beyond most people's dreams yet a young impoverished woman had achieved more than she ever had. Surprisingly, Cat s realized she not only admired Omri but envied the woman whose circumstances were challenging and required that she work extremely hard and persevered beyond all normal expectations. Along with all that she sacrificed all she could for her family.

Gerald would arrive soon and they would drive to Tony's in his brand new jet black Jaguar. As Cat slipped the icy blue dress over her head she pondered how Gerald would talk about his day and how he had once again put some poor employee in their place.

In fact, that is was just what happened as Gerald maneuvered his sports car at top speed weaving in and out of traffic. She listened attentively with a sweet smile, nodded often and sympathized with him.

When they arrived at Tony's valet parking and Gerald offhandedly asked her about her day she answered with, "I finished my work on the reception area project for the Branson hotel yesterday, so today was a day off. I bought this dress from Nichole's shop and had lunch with Liv at Chez Paris."

Gerald smiled, handed the keys to the uniformed valet attendant and commented, "Sounds like you had an easy day off."

He gazed at Cat with appreciation as they walked into the dining area and gushed with pride when heads turned to look at her. She looked stunning in the blue dress. He liked the way men glanced covetously at her and women stared at her in envy. After tonight, Cat would be all his.

The waiter smiled and ushered them to their table. Gerald ordered White Merlot, Cat's favorite. The attentive waiter returned with their drinks, relayed the list of house specials and handed them their menus.

Cat gazed across the table at Gerald as they toasted, took a sip of wine and glanced down at her menu. Gerald got a message on his cell phone and was texting rapidly.

"Sorry babe," he apologized, "no one can make a decision without me."

Cat smiled back and returned to her menu. The truth was Gerald was fortunate to have a staff of experienced I.T. professionals who could easily run his company. Most of the time he was with CEO's having power lunches at the club or attending important meetings on the golf course.

Suddenly, a sound akin to a harsh scratching of a record at a rave concert pierced her senses. A sick revelation hit her like the clamping of a Venus Fly Trap on its unsuspecting victim.

Cat realized that she did not love Gerald Abernathy Tiergarten II, not one bit. No amount of money or prestige or pedigree would change that. In fact her real excitement had been about being in love. She realized that in the past she wouldn't have been able to recognize real love if it knocked her flat on her rear.

A vision of Omri bending over her sleeping son and the look on her face swelled Cat's heart with emotion. That was real love; unvarnished, sweaty exhausting, self-sacrificing love. Working 16 hours a day to help put her husband through medical school, and her patience with her mother-in-law was true love and devotion.

Gerald never did a loving thing in his life. He wouldn't even pass a few bucks to a homeless man on the street. He walked right past every red kettle in the city at Christmas time. When she broke her ankle on a skiing trip earlier that year, he was so helpless and uncomfortable in the ER he had to disappear claiming he needed to get a drink, which was a big swig of vodka from the sliver flask always present in his pocket.

Cat excused herself to the lady's room and stood at the mirror. Tears threatened to flow down her cheeks. She wiped her face with a tissue and reapplied her lipstick. How she wanted to be a little girl again and run to her mother to be held. Sadly, her mother would hand her off to her nanny, Tanya. It was she who comforted her when she was sick. She gave her first aid when she fell on her knees after her first bike ride. Tanya really loved her. Her brown arms were always ready to embrace her. She still sent her a card every Christmas and on her birthday. The yearly cards always included photos of Tanya's 5 children at various stages of growth.

When Cat walked back to the table Gerald smiled at her and asked, "Everything ok?" When she nodded he continued, "Let's order I'm starved. The filet mignon looks good."

She finally realized that Gerald never looked at her with love in his eyes but territorial possession, like he had just scored a big coup. Not one ounce of unbridled passion showed on his face. He probably figured once he handed her the sparkling diamond engagement ring she would be his. Why work at it?

When Cat rose from her chair again, Gerald looked up at her with irritation more than surprise. He was about question her but Cat leaned down, kissed him on the cheek and whispered, "Goodbye, Gerald."

Cat walked away with a slight smile and did not look back. Of course, Gerald did not call out, "Cate don't go!" Perhaps if he had there might have been a second chance.

That night Cat lay under her fluffy comforter, clutching her stuffed puppy, Tanya had given her as a child. She wondered what her life would have been like if she hadn't seen that icy blue dress in Nichole's shop. She suddenly felt very cold and pulled the covers closer to her.

Cat shuddered. She was convinced she had narrowly escaped the ravenous jaws of a lion. Swallowed down that gaping throat Cat would disappear and become, Mrs. Gerald Abernathy Tiergarten II.

The Big Freeze

The Big Freeze

I was driving west on I-44 about five miles from St. James, Missouri when my Prius stalled. I coasted briefly and pulled on the tiny shoulder of the highway and narrowly escaped sliding into a drainage ditch that abutted a farmer's field.

Two hours from St. Louis a winter storm had pelted the interstate with wind, snow and ice. I took a deep breath and pulled out my cell phone. To my surprise it had lost its charge and my phone charger was out of juice. I realized then that the battery was the problem not the engine. The gas tank was half full before I stalled.

Frustrated, I pounded on my steering wheel and growled like very angry lioness. I calmed myself down and pondered what my options were. I could stay in the car and pile on the blankets and comforter I had stowed in my suitcase for a weekend stay with my parents, or I could get out, bundle up and hoof it to town. Neither choice was ideal because they all ended with me turning into a human pop-sickle. I opted for the latter. I fully intended to go down fighting. I tended to be very melodramatic when imminent death was near.

I added two sweatshirts under my winter coat, zipped it up to within an inch of strangulation, lowered my hat to just above my eyebrows, and wrapped a knit scarf around my neck two times. I doubled my knee socks and stuffed my feet into my snow boots.

I retrieved the flashlight from the glove compartment, climbed out of the car and locked the doors. I didn't quite understand my

101

motivation for this since the locks were going to freeze solid in about twenty minutes anyway. I pocketed my keys and surveyed the road.

It was three in the morning and New Year's Day. I had left at two am hoping to beat the snowstorm that I knew was heading for western Missouri. Happy New Year's Day to unlucky me! Of course the highway was deserted everyone in their right mind was sleeping off their champagne or other celebratory drinks.

As I walked up the highway on the icy shoulder, I felt like the last woman on earth in a very bad post-apocalyptic climate change sci-fi movie. Progress was slow and treacherous. I commandeered a tree branch that had fallen onto the shoulder and used it as a walking stick.

The pavement was mostly snow covered so I had a bit of leverage for my footing. My snow boots gave me the traction I needed not to wipe out and brain myself on the asphalt.

Now, for the bad part, the wind howled and whipped blowing snow right into my face. My glasses fogged up and I had to keep wiping them with my gloves.

Fortunately, with the heavy snow the temperature had risen to about 30 degrees, according to the news report I had checked on my phone before it died. I did not try to guess the wind chill temperature at the moment. Hysterics do not go well while hiking on slick roads.

I was elated to see Bob's Gasoline Alley to my right. Bob's was one of my favorite highway landmarks on the way to St. James. It was an interesting compound with lots of colorful old gas station billboard signs plastered across its left boundary line. This night it was enhanced with colorful giant Christmas lights on stakes.

Bob's was also an exotic animal farm. In the warmer months travelers literally pulled over on the shoulder to take pictures of the emu's, antelopes, donkeys, sheep, long horned steer, bison, llamas and alpacas.

The gas station and other buildings were about a fourth of a mile up the hill. I didn't expect to see the animals in the field, not in this frigid snowy weather. I could picture them all huddled up in their stalls, cozy and warm in their heated barns.

I decided to head for the main building, call a tow truck and my parents. Climbing the wooden fence around the property was not an easy task for a short lady bundled up so thick she resembled a fat blue snowman. I finally reached the top horizontal slat and rolled over it onto the soft snow. I laughed out loud at how ridiculous I must have looked, brushed off the powdery snow and headed across the field, at as good a clip as I could go in 2 feet of snow. I had one goal. "Gimme Shelter"!

Halfway across the range, I heard a strange snorting sound to my right. I pointed the flashlight in that direction and what I saw made me weak in the knees. A very large and angry long-horned bull was bellowing and pawing the ground with his front hooves.

The bull froze a moment in the bright flashlight beams and I veered to the left and ran for my life as fast as I could up the hill. My boots were kicking up snow clouds like a snowmobile in high gear.

When I turned to look, the bull was charging clumsily in the snowdrifts grinding up the ground like a snowplow tractor with a stuck accelerator.

Up ahead I could see a small wooden display hut used to sell grapes and other fruits to tourists. I made a beeline for the building. It was all uphill now and my legs were pumping so hard my knees were nearly hitting my chin.

I could almost feel the bull's hot breath on my back as if it was right behind me and closing. It had to be close at my heels. I kept veering right, then left, so I wouldn't give him an easy target.

I made it to the shed and rolled over the counter and shut the overhead sliding door. Peering through a hole in the plastic I could see that the bull had stopped a few yards away. I was just about to give a sigh of relief when the crazed animal charged the stand.

As I rolled up into a ball on the floor near the back wall of the stand, both of the bull's long horns pierced the sliding door and stuck, right above my head. This made the bull madder than a hornet. He snorted and blew hot breath out like a bellows.

I noticed that the stand had a side door for the seller to enter. I rammed into the door until it burst opened and fell to the ground from the impetus. I darted behind the stand and headed up the hill to the main building.

As I expected, the gas station was closed for the holiday. I wiped condensation from the window and spied a telephone on the counter. I pushed and rammed into the door but it didn't budge. I didn't care if I set off an alarm as long as help came.

By this time the bull had freed himself and was sniffing and scanning the area for me. I scurried around the building in the dark not wanting to use my flashlight. I nearly ran into a large trash dumpster.

The bull must have smelled my fear, because I could hear him pouncing and pawing around the building. Without much thought I lifted the dumpster lid, grabbed the metal lip and pulled myself up until I could lean forward enough to drop inside. I landed on a plastic bag filled with trash that cushioned my fall.

The dumpster was dark and icy cold but I dared not move or turn on my flashlight. I heard the bull bellowing again but the sound was further away. I lifted the lid a fraction of an inch and saw that he had backed up to get a head start on his next stampede. He was a smart old bull and knew I was inside. He could smell me. Heck, I could smell me I was sweaty with fear.

I got as far down in the dumpster and as close to its back wall as I could and piled all the bags on top me. Suddenly the bull rammed the dumpster. The sound was deafening like someone hitting a pot with a spoon right next to your ear. The container was pushed off its moorings and slid onto the snow.

Gritting my teeth, I waited for the inevitable ram complete with horns, but it never came. Even though the dumpster kept the wind out, I was so cold I thought I would pass out. It was unfathomable to me that this dumpster should become my stinky tomb. I was determined to live. I had a husband and two children to think about.

Somewhere on this road there had to be a house, and people to help me. I waited a few more minutes lifted the lid. To my amazement, the bull was not in sight. I checked the immediate area with my flashlight to make sure.

Flipping the dumpster lid back, I tentatively pulled myself up and over, this time landing on my feet.

I began to wonder about my encounter with the long horn. Had he been real or a Native American spirit wondering the snow covered fields. When I stepped in something squishy and soft I realized the animal had been real, for he had left a steaming pile of dung.

I wiped my boots clean in the snow and decided to walk back to the highway. The snow had stopped and the silvery moon broke brightly through the white puffy clouds. It guided my way back down the hill. I climbed back over the fence and to my car.

The Prius was frozen and still. I managed to get the door open using the key hidden in the key fob. I tried the engine but the battery was still dead and probably frozen by now too.

My teeth began to chatter and I couldn't feel my feet. Running did not work. My legs were like two stiff poles. I wondered how it felt to die in the cold. Did you feel excruciating pain as your muscles slowly freeze and your blood congeal? Did you finally go to sleep and never wake up?

Incredibly thirsty, I grabbed a handful of snow and sucked on it until it melted and I could swallow it. I hadn't had anything to drink and my stomach growled with hunger. I guess I wanted to live more than tumble to the ground and die. My body surely did.

A light up ahead lifted my spirits and I hobbled toward it. I must have been whimpering aloud because I spooked a tiny rabbit and it darted away from me. My eyes watered and the tears started to solidify on the way down my cheeks.

I panted and trudged further and further but the light got no closer. I realized that the light I so desperately sought was merely a star twinkling close to the moonlit horizon. There were no houses in sight, no barns, no shacks, nothing. I was trekking in a wasteland, forgotten, abandoned and left for dead.

My mind lost its focus I started fantasizing about warm fires, bonfires, erupting volcanoes, even the fires of hell, anything to keep warm. My whole being wanted to lie down and curl into a ball and just let go.

It was my spirit and love for family that made me slap myself awake. I told myself that one day I would look back at this and laugh. I scolded myself for giving up when it was only a matter of minutes and I would make it to the exit ramp for St. James.

Something up ahead looked familiar. I skated through the drifts to get a closer look. My heart fell. I was back at Bob's Gasoline Alley. In my dazed state I had turned around and walked in the opposite direction. I kicked at the snow and let out a primal scream. How could I be so stupid? I was a goner now for sure.

I looked up at the night sky and shook my fist. I guess I was mad at God but it wasn't his fault my car battery died. I was a victim of circumstances not his wrath. There was nothing left to do but to turn around and walk the right way.

As if by a miracle, I heard a noise behind me. I turned and saw the bright headlights of an eighteen wheeler. I waved my flashlight at the trucker and yelled for him to stop.

The big rig stopped, the driver leaned over the seat of the cab rolled down the window. I must have looked pretty pathetic because he said, "Hop in little lady. Looks like I got here just in time. You're half frozen."

"Thanks," I said as he grabbed my arm and helped me into the cab.

"Was that your little Prius back there?" the trucker asked, "Terrible cars in this weather."

I was so happy to be warm again I didn't protest his rude remark. My feet, face and hands were finally thawing out. They stung and burned but I realized I was going to make it out alive.

The driver was burly, and appeared to be in his fifties. He had a swarthy bearded face and dark blue eyes with a friendly smile that displayed perfect white teeth. Under his warm Alpine work jacket, He wore a red and black plaid lumber jack shirt. His hands on the wheel were knobby and work worn.

He turned to me and asked, "Where can I drop you off little miss?"

"St. James if you would be so kind," I answered, returning his smile.

The driver nodded and said, "No problem."

He turned back and started the engine. The full moon overhead followed us as we sped down the highway.

I looked out the side view mirror at his beautiful rig. It was shiny stainless steel with bright running lights and moved quietly like a streamlined land cruiser.

Suddenly, in the dim light of the cab, I noticed a change come over the driver. At first I thought it was the odd shadows inside the cab made by the swaying air fresheners that hung from his inside mirror. His head seemed to become more hairy, his nose more elongated, and dark curly hair covered his long knobby fingers. I hadn't noticed before how long his fingernails were.

I shook with fear not cold. I swallowed hard and tried not to look at the man. I stared straight ahead. When I noticed the green sign "St. James 5 miles," I peeked at the driver. He was grinning, his mouth opened, he bared his long pointed teeth and razor sharp incisors. Saliva dripped down his chin onto his shirt.

The driver slowed down at the turn off and made it up the exit ramp. When he hit the brakes before he turned, I leaped out of the truck and shouted as I ran away. "Thanks but I think I'll walk the rest of the way!" He drove by me, slowed down and waved. He opened his window, stuck out his head and howled up at the moon.

I kept running and didn't look back as I neared my parent's street. I thought to myself some situations are worse than being in a deep freeze. There are certainly worse ways to go.

Who Killed Doc Robbins?

Who Killed Doc Robbins?

*G*inny paused at the door of the Olivette Veterinary Center, looked down at her red-bone coon hound and said, "Holmes, mind your manners and you'll get one of Doc's dog bones. We're only here to get your heartworm pills, not your shots."

Holmes looked up at his mistress with large luminous brown eyes and cocked his head. "Shots, did she say shots?" he asked himself. He was very nervous. Sometimes when they came to this place the nice man jabbed him with something sharp, then apologized. He lowered his cinnamon colored head and obediently followed his mistress into the clinic.

When Ginny entered the office, she saw that Doc's Assistant, Colleen, wasn't at her desk. She gazed down the short hall and called, "Colleen! Doc! Is anybody here?"

Ginny walked down the corridor, cane in one hand and her dog's leash in the other. The first thing Doc Robbins would notice was the cane. She would have to tell him that she had recently been diagnosed with MS. Doc would be concerned, put his arm around her and say something like, "You'll get through this Ginny. You're one of the strongest women I know."

Doc had been her vet and friend for 20 years. He had taken care of her Shepherd-Collie Bambino for 15 years. He had been the one to put him down, with tears in his eyes. 5 years later he became in charge of her largest canine yet, Holmes.

Doc had warned her when she brought in the three month old hound for his first visit and saw the huge paws on the little puppy. He had let out a whistle and said, "This one might make the Guinness book of Records." Doc had studied the cute little puppy's bone structure, grinned and exclaimed, "I think we have rediscovered The Hound of the Baskervilles! Sir Arthur Conan Doyle would be proud!"

Halfway down the hall Holmes looked up at Ginny and whimpered. He sat down in the middle of the floor and refused to budge.

Ginny patted his head and ordered "Stay. I just want to say hello to Doc. I'll be right back."

She entered the first examination room on the right and gasped. Feeling weak in the knees, she leaned onto her cane to steady herself.

Doc was slumped over the shiny, stainless steel examining table. His body was twisted at an odd angle. Ginny quickly felt for his pulse. Nothing, not even a faint heart beat registered on her fingers. Tears filled her soft hazel eyes as she scanned his body. Walking around the table, she noticed a large contusion on the left side of his head. Blood had congealed on his scalp and hair, yet the blood droplets that had dripped onto the floor hadn't. He had died within the last hour.

Ginny saw something under his lab coat collar that made her cringe. A syringe was stuck in the side of Doc's neck. Her trained eyes surveyed the room. A discarded bottle had been dropped into the medical waste can. She took out her cell phone and used the flashlight to look at the bottle. It was an empty bottle of animal tranquilizer.

She leaned against the counter as unchecked tears rolled down her cheeks and dialed 911. Help would come soon. The Olivette Police Station was right across the street. Ginny took photos of the crime scene and the discarded bottle and stored them on her phone.

Ginny led Holmes back to the waiting room. She called Father John at Holy Cross Church. Doc and his family were devout Catholics and he would have wanted to be given the last rites.

Calling Doc's wife would be the job of Doc's long-time friend, Police Chief Jackson.

Unable to breathe, Ginny left the clinic to get some much needed fresh air. While she waited she took out her memo pad to write down detailed notes. As the prime witness at the murder scene, she wanted to remember exactly what she saw. Having been married to a police officer for 28 years, she knew the procedures that had to be followed.

When her husband, Jordan, had been killed four years ago in the line of duty, Doc had been there for her. He attended Jordan's funeral and offered to take care of Holmes so she could make arrangements. Doc Robbins cared about the town pets and its people.

Ginny bent to hug Holmes and whispered, "Who would want to kill such a wonderful vet and kind man?"

Holmes knew his mistress was sad and gently licked her face. He tasted her salty tears and rested his large head on her chest near her beating heart.

Ginny stood up and inhaled the fresh morning air. She noticed an elderly lady with a cane in one hand and an empty pet carrier in the other walking toward the clinic.

Halting her progress, Ginny stated, "Ma'am you can't go in there right now. Dr. Robbins has had an emergency and had to cancel his appointments."

The woman stared at her coldly, "Where is Colleen? I never heard of such a thing. I came to get my cat, Marbles."

"You'll get your kitty tomorrow," Ginny insisted, "Now please go back home and call tomorrow."

The ancient woman shook her cane at her, "You tell Robbins when you see him I'm not paying for today's boarding!"

Ginny watched as the woman made her way back to her car. She backed slowly out of her parking space and glared at Ginny until she was out of sight.

Ginny shook her head and refused to let the old woman rattle her. She went to her car, let Holmes in, lowered herself into the front seat, and waited.

Seeing Doc murdered had triggered a flashback of her husband's death. Two good men had been ripped from the earth before their time. She could do nothing to solve her husband's murder and the police never found his killer, but she vowed to do all she could to find Doc's murderer.

Ginny got back out of the car when she saw Colleen walking up the sidewalk toward the clinic carrying two cups of coffee and a bag of Ray's doughnuts.

"Colleen, wait!" she exclaimed. Ginny caught up with her as she stopped in front of the clinic. "Don't go in there!"

Seeing Ginny's stricken expression Colleen asked, "Why? What's wrong? Have we been robbed?"

Ginny stammered, "Colleen, something's happened to Doc."

The cardboard tray with two cups of hot coffee and a bag of doughnuts tipped crazily and dropped to the ground. Colleen gave a strangled cry and ran into the clinic.

Ginny tried to catch up with her but her legs would not cooperate. She got to the examining room just as Colleen saw Doc's body.

Colleen gave a horrified cry and Ginny grabbed her before she crumpled onto the floor. She walked her back to the waiting room and sat her down on a chair.

"I can't believe it! I was only gone about 15 minutes!" Colleen exclaimed shaking her head.

The sound of sirens in the parking lot signaled the arrival of the police. The forensic van pulled right behind them in front of the clinic door. The officers quickly cordoned off the area and moved people away from the scene.

Chief Jackson entered the clinic and walked over to Ginny and Colleen, "I'm sorry you two ladies had to find Doc like that," he tipped his cap and added, "I need to go in there and have a look at him."

He turned toward Colleen, "Colleen, I want you to get all the pet owner's records and download them from the computer. Officer Ellen Masters will be here in a few minutes to take your statement and make sure you get home safely."

The Chief's face displayed controlled emotions. He and Doc had been best friends. They grew up in the same neighborhood, a tough neighborhood on the north side. They watched each other's backs all through grade school and high school.

Ginny noted his determined expression as he started down the hall. She recognized that look. It's the same look Jordan had on his face when he was searched for suspects, "perps" as he had called them.

Ginny touched his arm as he went by, "Don't worry Chief, Colleen and I will be okay. Let me know what else I can do to help."

Colleen looked up at the Chief and murmured through her tears, "Me too, Chief, anything for Doc." Her voice faded and tears streamed down her cheeks.

Doc had been a life saver for Colleen. Twenty years earlier she had made a terrible mistake. She had driven her boyfriend and his brother to a liquor store and waited while they committed a robbery. When the police came and arrested the two boys, she fled the scene. She was arrested later that day after the two boys had given her up under questioning. They blamed the robbery on her. The judge didn't accept their explanation but Colleen was convicted for participating in the crime. She had no previous record, and because she was still a juvenile she was sentenced to community service and had to wear an ankle bracelet for a year.

Colleen's juvenile officer had told her about a program called, "Second Chances." Doc Robbins was part of the program. When she turned 18, he had offered her a job as an Administrative Assistant for his new practice. Doc had paid for a computer course and given her a decent salary. Because Doc trusted her, she stayed and had never looked back.

The clinic bell jingled again. It was Father John in priestly garb. He carried his Bible, a prayer book for the Last Rites and a small case containing holy oils. He nodded to the Chief, and gave his sincere condolences to Colleen and Ginny.

Father John proceeded to the examining room where Dr. Ramsey, the coroner was examining Doc's body. They heard the priest's gentle voice as he prayed, "Dear Lord, receive the soul of

Donald Robbins into your heavenly kingdom, in the name of the Father, the Son and the Holy Spirit."

Dr. Ramsey halted Father John and called for the Chief. He complained that he was destroying the crime scene by giving Doc the Last Rites.

Chief Jackson took the coroner aside and Ginny heard their heated discussion all the way in the waiting room.

As a result of their conference, the coroner conceded that the Last Rites could be administered when he was finished with his examination and photos.

Officer Ellen Masters entered the clinic and greeted the two women. She took their statements and Colleen handed her the zip drive downloaded with patient records. Her patient and empathetic manner put both women at ease.

After the interviews, Chief Jackson sat next to Ginny and said, "Ginny go to the diner and have some hot sweet tea and order some of those croissants you like, on me. I'll be by later and we'll talk, okay?"

"Sure, Chief," Ginny agreed, "I'm too shaky to drive home right now anyway."

Father John left the clinic and offered Ginny his arm. He walked her to the diner saying, "Ginny, I can't believe it. I know I should offer you words of comfort but I'm stunned right now. I can't fathom why anyone would kill Don. It's a clear example of using one's free will to do evil. My faith assures me that Don has received his reward, but I'm still heartbroken that he is gone." He paused and held the door open saying, "Go ahead, I'll be back in a few minutes."

Once in the diner, Ginny walked past worried patrons who had heard the sirens and watched as the coroner's van parked in front of the clinic.

A few moments later, The Chief entered the room and nodded to Ginny. Before he sat down, he stood in the middle of the diner and gave the patrons a brief summary of what happened and finished with, "Please go back to your breakfasts and if you saw or heard anything when you came here this morning please let us know. Officer Masters will be outside to take your statements."

Barb, their server, came to their table brushed tears from her eyes and took their order. Chief Jackson ordered a pot of black coffee and two bacon egg and cheese bagels. Ginny sipped her tea and ordered a raspberry croissant.

A few minutes later, the Chief thanked Barb for the coffee and poured some into his large ceramic cup. He took a drink, caught Ginny's eye, and said, "I know you gave your statement to Ellen but did you see anyone around after you discovered Doc's body?"

Ginny nodded, "I did see an elderly woman. She looked to be in her 70's. She was very skinny like a strong wind could knock her over. She used one of those canes with a tripod stand on the end. It's a miracle she could walk let alone lug a cat carrier in the other hand. She had on a flimsy housedress and wore a tattered winter coat over it. She had on good walking shoes, Dr. Scholl's, I think."

The Chief nodded, "Very observant. Go ahead."

"I told her there had been an emergency and Doc had cancelled all his appointments for the day," Ginny stated then continued, "She gave me a dirty look and said she came to pick up her cat, Marbles. I told her to call tomorrow and she could arrange a time to pick it up. She glared at me and demanded I tell Doc that she was not going to pay for the extra day's boarding."

"I'll go over your statement with Ellen later," Chief Jackson said. He looked at Ginny's still wan face. Dark circles lay under her grief stricken eyes. "Ginny, how are you feeling?"

"Right now I'm shocked and heartbroken about Doc," she answered, "If you are asking about my MS I'm adjusting to the injections and a lovely cocktail of various drugs. They seem to be helping. I still need a cane to steady my right leg which is the worse of the two and I get tired too quickly but it could be worse. I could be in a wheel chair."

Father John joined them a few minutes later and Barb brought his usual breakfast; two eggs sunny side up, two slices of bacon, hash browns and wheat toast. The three friends had a comforting discussion about Doc. They reminisced about what a good friend, husband and member of his church and the community he had been his whole life.

After breakfast Chief Jackson waved goodbye as Father John walked Ginny back to her car. The priest looked at her and asked, "Are you okay to drive?"

"Yes, Father, and thanks," Ginny responded.

After they said a prayer for Doc and his family, Ginny got in her car and drove home. Holmes, who had fallen asleep in the car, woke up and nuzzled Ginny with his wet nose as she pulled into their driveway. She petted the dog and opened the door to their two-story home. He gobbled down the two strips of bacon Father John had saved for him, took a drink of water and ran to the back door.

Ginny sat in the glider on the back deck while Holmes sprinted into the yard, attended to his bodily functions and chased away the squirrels who loved to chase each other around the trunk of the large walnut tree in the back yard.

She breathed in the sweet spring air and gazed at the myriad of flowers that grew in her two side gardens that bordered the wooden shadow box fence. There were tulips of red, bright yellow, orange, peachy pink, myriads of daffodils in white and bright yellow and purple hyacinths. A large statue of St. Francis of Assisi holding a bird bath stood in front of the flowering bushes in the back garden.

Her heart was filled with longing for her husband Jordan who would often sit next to her on the glider and hold her hand. As she observed the amazing beauty surrounding her, she wondered aloud, "God, how can I sit here and admire the beauty of my gardens when my dear friend Doc was so brutally murdered? Is that why you gave us flowers, trees and birds, so we wouldn't sink into complete despair?" Tears rolled down her cheeks, "Please help me bring Doc's killer to worldly justice. I'll leave the heavenly judgement in your hands."

On a conference call with her two sons, Jordan Jr and Matt, Ginny told them about Doc's death. Both the boys had loved Doc

Robbins. Jordan Jr. had worked at the clinic two summers as a dog walker and pet care assistant.

Both of her sons attended the University of Missouri in Columbia. Jordan Jr. was in his final year of the 6 year M. D. program specializing in psychiatry, and Matt was almost finished with his bachelor's degree in criminal justice. They made plans to drive home this weekend to attend Doc's funeral services and spend their spring break with her.

After talking to her two sons, Ginny went to her office, sat down at her computer and downloaded the photos of the crime scene she had taken before she called the police. Ginny cringed when the photo of Doc's slumped over body came into view. She tried to study them objectively as her husband Jordan might have.

As she jotted down details of the scene she felt as if Jordan's spirit were right in the room with her, saying, "Come on babe, shake it off. You can do this."

It was clear that Doc had been facing the examining table when he was hit on the side of his head with a blunt object. He fell onto the stainless steel table which supported the lower half of his body as he slumped over. She zoomed the head shot and realized that Doc's head injury probably wasn't what killed him, but it had incapacitated him enough for the killer to load the ketamine into a syringe and administer the fatal dose directly into his carotid artery.

Ginny took a sip of coffee and wondered aloud, "Why would Doc stand in front of the examining table unless he was with a patient?"

Holmes who had been dozing under the desk looked up at her with soulful questioning eyes. Ginny patted his head and scratched him behind his ears and he settled back down with a contented sigh.

Ginny guessed that whoever killed Doc had timed it just right. Colleen had left the office to get their morning coffee and bagels from the diner. Doc was probably examining a pet that had been kept overnight when he was attacked from behind. No other drugs were stolen so it wasn't a robbery that became deadly. Obviously someone had a deep seated grudge against Doc.

The only way she was going to help solve this crime was to join the homicide team as a consultant, something she had done when Jordan was alive. She had a Master's degree in criminology and taught a Criminal Justice class at St. Louis Community College. She called Chief Jackson and shared her analysis of the case but he was reticent to enlist her help.

"That is not a good idea Ginny," stated, "Haven't you been through enough? Doc was your friend. You can't be objective about this case."

"Can you be objective?" Ginny retorted, "Yet, you have not excused yourself from the case. You and Doc have been friends since third grade."

"Well, I don't know," Chief Jackson wavered.

"And, this "is" personal, for both of us," Ginny insisted, "Some deranged person snuffed the life out of our friend! Don't deny me this. I'm qualified and I'm good at this job."

"Jordan always said you were the brains of the outfit," Chief Jackson commented.

Ginny clinched her position by using his given name, "You owe me this Taylor. Let's do it for Jordan, he loved Doc too. My husband was the best detective you had and I was right behind him all the way. Let's put this psycho away forever!"

"All right, but I was convinced at 'this is personal'," Chief Jackson admitted. "Jordan always said you were pushy."

"Tenacious," Ginny corrected, "he said I was tenacious."

"Yeah, that too," Chief Jackson stated wryly, "Be here tomorrow morning nine sharp and bring those photos and notes I know you have," He concluded with, "and get some sleep will you?"

"I'll try, I promise," Ginny answered, "Thanks Chief."

Back at home, Ginny rose from her chair and turned off her computer. It was 7pm and she had to fix something to eat for herself and Holmes who was pacing back and forth excitedly as she walked into the kitchen.

It was nearly midnight when she put her notes away and climbed into bed. Holmes was already curled up in his favorite spot with his head on Jordan's old pillow. He had planted himself there after her husband's funeral and Ginny didn't have the heart to order him to go to his bed. Besides he was a soft, warm, furry presence to replace the cold nothingness left behind when Jordan was killed.

The following morning the homicide team drank coffee and munched on Croissants and bagels from the Olivette Diner while they poured over the forensic and physical evidence of Doc's murder.

Ginny's eyes were peeled to the patient logs Colleen had sent over on zip drive. Curiously, there had been no appointments scheduled before 10 am the morning of Doc's murder.

When she studied Colleen's statement, she found that it was not unusual for the clinic to have walk-ins. Emergencies happened, clients stopped in for pet supplies. As Colleen had stated, Doc was always ready to help an animal, even if they were not a regular patient of his.

Ginny dialed Colleens home number and said, "Colleen, this it Ginny. Did Doc have any problems dealing with animal abuse?"

Colleen paused a moment to think and answered, "There was this case about a year ago. A woman brought in a sick cat. Poor little thing was in deplorable condition, malnourished riddled with disease, near death really. Doc treated the calico for nothing. I've never heard him raise his voice in anger until that day. He threatened to report her Animal Welfare for the State of Missouri if she ever brought in another animal in that condition again."

"How did the woman react," Ginny asked.

"She told Doc to mind his own business and ranted that she took good care of all her babies. The woman took her cat and stormed out of the clinic yelling that she would find another doctor if she needed help."

"Do you have any information on the woman?' Ginny questioned.

"Doc didn't ask for it but I'm sure he must have written down the medications he had given the cat,' Colleen responded then added, "I remember, he sent her home with some sample pain meds, vitamins and a 10-pound bag of cat food, free of charge."

"Did the woman ever call Doc again?" Ginny asked.

"I'll check the call record," Colleen promised, "I always send it to my e-mail in case Doc calls me after clinic hours."

"Thanks Colleen. Just send me a text when you find it," Ginny requested. "Take care, girlfriend."

Ginny took a sip of coffee, rechecked her notes and looked over at Ellen, "Colleen, I may have a name for us."

Ellen smiled and said, "I hope so because I haven't gotten any e-mail from the state reporting any abuse of a calico in our area."

Ginny's phone buzzed. It was Colleen, "I found something in last June, "she stated in an excited voice, "I wrote down the name Patches for the calico and the owner's name was Mavis. It has to be the same woman. She didn't give me her last name." Colleen paused a moment, "Oh this is interesting I jotted down that she was wanted to know what the cost of neutering a Great Dane would be. Yes, I remember this woman now. When I told her what the cost would be, she called it highway robbery and hung up."

"Is there anyone else that might have had an issue with Doc?" Ginny asked.

Colleen hesitated then answered, "This wasn't exactly an issue. There was this client who accidentally backed over his pit bull puppy. The poor little thing had squeezed under the gate and hidden under the front wheels of the man's car. Several neighbors saw the whole thing. One called the police but verified to the responding officer that it was an accident. The owner wrapped the puppy in a blanket and brought him to the clinic. Doc couldn't save him. He had to put him down. We were all in tears."

"How awful," Ginny commented, "Thanks, I'll have Ellen question him but I don't think he would come after Doc for something like that."

Ginny thanked Colleen and hung up. So far except for the calico owner the leads were not promising. She mulled over her notes and reports for several hours.

Chief Jackson caught sight of her still at the desk and motioned for her to come into his office. He looked at her tired face and said, "Go home Ginny take a break and get some rest."

"Probably a good idea, I've got to take my medicines and I have to rest afterwards," Ginny agreed.

Ginny pondered the case on the drive home. She stopped to get a salad from Wendy's and made her way home. Holmes would appreciate the extra order of grilled chicken she got for him.

After taking her medicines and administering her shot, she ate her lunch at the kitchen café table and gazed out the large many-paned window at the garden.

Holmes sniffed at her feet and she gave him his grilled chicken treats. She pushed her chair away from the table and he jumped up to be petted. He took a drink of water and his ears perked up when she got out his favorite toy, a stuffed hedgehog called Buda and tossed it into the hall.

She got up and moved stiffly. It always took an hour for the medication to work. In the meantime she walked like an old lady with severe arthritis.

An idea hit her like a bolt of lightning and she punched the table so hard Holmes ran over to see if she was okay. "It's all right boy, mom just got an idea!" Holmes cocked his head. She could swear he was grinning up at her.

Ginny sat in the living room on her recliner and put up her aching feet. She took out her notepad and read the description of the older lady that showed up at Doc's to pick up her cat.

She texted Colleen asking, "Colleen, did you board a cat in the clinic the night before Doc was killed?"

"Yes," Collen texted, "the technician left about an hour ago. All the animals were to be picked up until after the funeral. There was a neutered dog, a bunny to be delivered to the humane society; an Easter gift that didn't work out, and a black cat."

"Can you find out who picked up the cat?" she texted back.

"I'll call Denny and text you back," Colleen replied.

Ginny put down her notes and leaned back on the recliner part of her sectional. As she dozed off Holmes jumped up next to her on his blanket and joined her.

An hour later a musical text notice from her phone woke her up. She grabbed her phone to read what it said. It was from

Colleen, she let her know that an old lady had picked up the cat right before closing time. Danny, the technician had worried he might have to take the cat home with him.

Convinced Doc's wife, Betty might know something about Mavis, Ginny called her. A family member picked up and said she was resting and not able to take calls.

"Please tell her Ginny Ballatore called," Ginny clicked off, somewhat deflated. A few minutes later her phone rang. It was Betty, Doc's wife.

"Ginny," Betty asked, "I heard you were helping Taylor to find my husband's killer. Thank God. How can I help?"

"Did Doc talk to you about a particularly horrific case of animal abuse?" Ginny asked then added, "This would have been last summer and it was about a cat."

"Yes, I've never seen him as upset with a client as he was with that old biddy," Betty answered, "He suspected her of pet hoarding. She lives outside of St. Charles in an unincorporated part of the county. Mostly woods a few small farms, and run down homes."

"What did Doc do?" Ginny asked.

"After he treated the cat, he took an early lunch and followed her back to her farm," Betty informed her."

Ginny furiously copied down notes as Betty continued, "He followed her to an old root cellar. When she opened the doors he heard animals whimpering and barking. He moved her out of the way and discovered five adult cats and dogs living in filth three of the female dogs had tiny puppies, half starved, barely moving. There were kittens too running all over the dark musty cellar."

"Did Doc threaten to report her?" Ginny asked

"No. After she yelled at him to get off her private property or she would call the police, he calmed her down," Betty explained, "He could see she was poverty stricken, could hardly feed herself let alone the animals."

"I don't know if I would have been so kind," Ginny stated.

"Don always felt that pet hoarding was an illness. He thought the woman needed help, not incarceration or the psych ward," Betty explained.

"What did Doc do?" Ginny asked softly.

"What he always does," Betty answered, "He helped. A team of volunteers from the Humane Society and the High School cleaned up the entire place. Tom's Hardware donated fencing for five dog runs with kennels. Don and the Veterinary Association of Missouri donated two fenced in compounds for the cats with an indoor area, litter boxes and heaters for the dog and cat kennels."

"Essentially Doc set her up with a good breeding business that would help her earn a living," Ginny commented.

"Exactly," Betty agreed, "All the animals were taken to area clinics and treated," Betty said, "No animals died."

"How did Mavis respond?" Ginny inquired.

"At first she was so grateful she couldn't stop thanking everyone," Betty told her, "Word got around and PetCo donated a year of food and supplies. There was a write up in the paper."

"Did Doc follow up with her this year?" Ginny asked.

"Not that I know of but if she walked in he would have helped her animals in a heartbeat, no charge," Betty answered.

"Thanks Betty you were a great help," Ginny stated, "Doc was a good friend to this whole town. What can I do to help?"

"You can see to it that the low life scum who murdered my husband is put behind bars!" Betty exclaimed, "And then you can have them throw away the key!"

Depressed and tired, Ginny spent the evening out on the patio, tossing Holmes his ball. When it got too dark to see, she gazed up at the moon and went inside. She refused to watch the news but opened her Bible and did her daily reading.

The next morning she quickly fed Holmes and hugged him goodbye. She stopped at the Olivette Diner and picked up breakfast sandwiches, coffee and doughnuts for the police crew.

Ginny handed Ellen a cup of coffee, offered her a sandwich and filled her in on what she had found out from Betty. Ellen called the owner of the crushed Pit Bull puppy. She signed off and relayed the information.

"I think we can check him off the suspect list. Mr. Cluney is happily raising a pit bull puppy, named Max. He also expressed his condolences about Doc. He mentioned that he had never received a bill from the clinic after his first puppy died."

"That is the kind of good man Doc was," Ginny stated."

She couldn't stop thinking about the old lady she had seen after Doc was killed. She looked over at Ellen and asked, "Did we ever contact the local Humane Society on Page?"

"No," we called the state association, but not the local business," Ellen replied, "What are you thinking?"

"Maybe they received complaints from neighbors or locals about Mavis's pet abuse," Ginny suggested.

"What's the plan?" Ellen asked eagerly.

"We could find out exactly where Mavis is hiding out these days and pay her a little visit." Ginny looked over at Ellen with a fire in her eyes and added, "Wouldn't it be great if we could solve Doc's murder before the funeral this weekend?"

Ellen's eyebrows arched, "That would be sweet!"

"If I'm right, all of Doc's help didn't change that old pet hoarder's M.O. one bit," Ginny stated.

Ellen picked up the phone and called the Humane Society on Page. After five minutes she hung up and threw up her fist, "Yes!"

"What did you find out?" Ginny asked excitedly.

"Not only did the neighbors complain," Ellen explained, "a door to door missionary worker reported her two weeks ago. The place was filthy, the kennels overrun with weeds and the animals looked like they were starving."

"What happened next?" Ginny asked hopefully.

"Last Friday, all the animals were removed from the premises and placed in no-kill rescue shelters to be taken care of until they could be put up for adoption," Ellen relayed, "and get this," she continued, "When the animal control officers went to collect the animals, Mavis went after one of the officers with her cane and tried to brain him!"

Both women looked at each other and said in unison, "The cane!" They had found Doc's killer. Mavis had used the cane to knock Doc senseless and then injected him with a lethal dose of ketamine.

"Why kill Doc?" Ellen asked.

"Mavis thought Doc turned her in," Ginny stated, "Remember, Colleen said he had threatened to turn her in last year when she brought in the calico."

"That stupid old cow," Ellen said enraged, "She killed Doc for nothing!"

"Well let's make sure her punishment is 'something'!" Ginny exclaimed.

"When did you start sounding like a cop?" Ellen asked.

"Twenty-eight years ago when I married one," Ginny said, "Now where is that hoarder's hell located?"

"Off ZZ, unincorporated St. Charles," Ellen informed her.

Ginny grabbed her purse and rose from her chair, "Come on, Ellen, you and I and that formidable sidearm of yours are going to catch a killer and animal abuser!"

It took about 45 minutes and Ellen's GPS on her police cruiser to navigate the winding roads and locate Mavis' farm. Ellen called in for backup as they pulled in the bumpy gravel drive.

The farm looked deserted as they exited the cruiser. Thankfully they heard no anguished animal cries as they were all safe and sound at the shelters.

"Ginny, stay behind me," Ellen ordered. She walked up to the rickety porch and knocked on the front door. When no one answered she raised her voice, "Open up it's the police. We would like to speak to Mavis."

Ginny saw a movement to her right out of the corner of her eye. Mavis rushed onto the porch with her cane poised over her head. This was not the weak bent old lady they had expected but an enraged mad woman. A strangled cry exploded from the woman's throat as she brought down her wooden cane. On reflex, Ginny instantly raised her metal cane and met Mavis's, with equal force. Mavis's own cane bounced back and hit her on the head. The old woman screamed, weaved dizzily and fell to the ground.

Ellen pulled the woman's arms behind her back and cuffed her. Chief Jackson arrived with sirens blaring as Ellen put Mavis in the back of the patrol car.

The Chief was fuming but happy to see both of the women. He read Mavis her rights and reported back to the station to cancel backup.

Ginny stared at Mavis through the window of the cruiser and said, "You pitiful old fool. Doc didn't report you. You killed the only person who ever tried to help you!"

Mavis stared back at her and howled, "They took my babies away! They took my babies!"

Ellen pulled Ginny away from the car, "That woman is looney tunes. Let's hope a shrink can straighten her up so she can stand trial and pay for killing Doc Robbins."

Chief Jackson scolded Ginny all the way back to the station for putting herself in harm's way. He turned to Ellen and scolded, "And you, Lt. Masters, if you ever pull a hair-brained stunt like that again you'll be walking the beat patrol at the mall the rest of your career!"

Ginny suppressed a grin and relaxed as they drove back to town. She and Ellen did a high five when the Chief wasn't looking. She prayed a silent prayer as they pulled into the station, "Lord, thank you for helping us find Doc's killer and bringing her to justice. Tell Doc we miss him!"

Dreamlife II

Dreamlife II

In his dimly lit bedroom, Connor, a boy of thirteen, stared intently at the screen of his computer. His right hand deftly manipulated the mouse while his left hand gripped the arm of his motorized wheel chair. He waited in breathless anticipation for the web site to come up.

In moments he would lose his corporeal form and enter into a second life. Beads of perspiration dotted his pale forehead and dampened his short brown hair. Excitement filled his dark eyes as he was transported to another place. His frustration and loneliness would soon melt away when he entered the cyber world of Dream Life II.

Connor's avatar, Xavier Dartanion, walked jauntily down the polished granite stairs of his ultra-modern manse of glass and titanium. Silver-framed Greco sunglasses covered his large cobalt blue eyes. His wide smile displayed his perfect white teeth. His coal black hair was smoothed back past his tanned forehead. Feathery black brows arched like raven's wings above his intelligent eyes. Beneath a long aquiline nose, Xavier's carefully trimmed mustache twitched as he slid into his gunmetal bronze Porsche and sped away.

The pale gray highway rose up to meet his shining car as he raced down the winding road. A panorama of scenery spread before him and expanded as his car climbed each hill; mansions, ranches, spas and castles surrounded by verdant hills, valleys and giant impossible trees of all colors, dotted the countryside of the

Peaceable Kingdom of Danthura. He drove past his own lands that boasted a vineyard, horse pastures, acres of cornfields, apple orchards and the meandering Moon River.

He slowed down in front of an elegant Victorian Manor, beeped the horn, and ordered his car to open the passenger door. His sister Elena's Avatar, Altara Star, the most famous singer in Danthura, stepped gracefully down the marble stairs, her waist length auburn hair moved in the light breeze. Her dark green eyes flashed happily in her heart-shaped face with its creamy flawless complexion. Her cheeks were rosy and her pink tinted bow mouth was turned up into a smile. As her tall, slender form slid into the passenger seat, she brushed her brother's cheek with a kiss.

Suddenly, a loud voice coming from above the purple mountains and azure skies broke their reunion. It called persistently, "Connor, Elena, dinner time! Come down and eat before it gets cold!"

It was their mother, Anna, who broke into their fantasy. Connor hit save, shut down his computer and grunted in irritation. He loved his mom but was reticent to stop the game just to eat.

Life seemed cruelly unfair to him. His wheelchair made a whirring sound as it moved down the hall to the stairway. His sister followed him to the stairs as he hooked his chair to the lift.

"Just when we were getting started," Connor complained.

"I know it's frustrating" Elena agreed, "Aren't you hungry?"

"I guess so," Connor stated as they descended the stairs back in the real world.

Anna met her children in the dining room. She carried steaming plates of chicken and rice and set them at their places. After they said grace, she turned to Connor, "Connor, remember our agreement. You can only spend two hours on your game after you finish your homework. You didn't check in with me before you started playing."

Connor looked down at his plate, "I know mom," he looked over at her and stated, "What else is there for a cripple to do." He saw the look of surprise on his mother's face and ignored his sister frantic "do not go there" shake of her head. "It's not like I can steel your car keys and drive myself to a rave downtown and drink myself into a stupor or something!"

"You are not a cripple!" his mother retorted. "You're a very brave and intelligent young man who should have better things to do than sit in front of a computer and waste your time in a dream world." Anna paused a moment then said, "Remember when we would gather around the table on weekends and play games together like Monopoly, Life and Scrabble? You loved to play Batman too."

"Mom, I was ten years old when we did that," Connor remarked, "I would wear a cape and walk around the room and pretend I could fly. Now I have to pretend I can walk! I can do anything on Dream Life II. I can swim under water or I can fly into space if I want to."

Connor's mom gazed over at Elena for support but she just stared at her plate. Anna looked over at her son with empathy, "But it's not real," she waved her hands around the room, "This is real what we have here and now. That world is a lie. The whole web site is artificial. Except for your sister, you shouldn't consider anyone else on Dream Life to be a true friend. In fact, be careful what you share with the other players."

It hurt Elena to see the pain in her mother's eyes. She spoke up saying, "I remember all the fun games we used to play when dad was alive. He would crack jokes about the characters in Clue like Col Mustard got drummed out of the army because he was too tangy! Mom, I understand why Connor likes Dream Life II. It helps both of us forget the past. Connor can forget the accident that killed dad and put him in a wheel chair."

Tears filled Anna's eyes and she nodded, "I guess I forgot how hard it is for both of you."

"Don't worry about Connor, mom," Elena said, "I'm right in the game with him. I'll make sure he doesn't get into trouble or get too obsessed."

Anna wiped her tears and took their plates. "I'm sorry if I was too harsh." She touched Connor's cheek and went into the kitchen to fill the dish washer.

Connor and Elena made their way upstairs to their rooms. As Connor rode the lift he gazed at his sister hopefully, "Elena, are we going to the rave on Danthura tonight?"

Elena smiled over at her brother, "I promised, didn't I? We have to finish our homework before bedtime though. I'll see you at nine, little brother, on the cyber side of life!"

Nine o' clock came and went as the siblings journeyed deep into Dream Life II. They rode to the rave in Xavier's sports car with its added neon running lights. The party was already in progress. Connor had missed his cyber friend Zander's spectacular entrance. He had landed earlier in his one-person, PASV, Personal Aerodynamic Stealth Vehicle.

The crowd begged Altara to get on stage and sing her new single, "Dangerous Cyber Love." While she belted out the torchy blues lyrics, she watched her brother as he conversed with a new avatar she had never met.

After Altara finished her song and bowed to the thundering applause, she motioned to Zander, asking, "Z, who is the tall dude in white?"

Zander took her hand to help her off the stage and replied, "He's called Preacher. He built the church on the hill." Zander walked to the window and pointed to the white building in the distance.

Altara gazed at the church in the distance. She turned back and studied the avatar called "Preacher." The tall stately man was dressed in a white suit with a white waistcoat and shining leather boots. He had a magnificent head of silvery white hair, a white mustache and deep gray iridescent eyes. Before she could make her way through the crowd, her brother and the stranger left the club and flew away.

She smiled and waved away the other avatars that greeted her and ran outside to see where Xavier flew off to. She was worried because her brother seemed to be mesmerized by Preacher.

Altara spotted her brother at the entrance to the church. Xavier waved to her and he and Preacher entered the tall red doors. Preacher turned back, looked at her with a smug look on his face and smiled. A chill went down her corporeal spine.

Two majestic live oaks grew on either side of the church building and shaded the muted green landscape. It seemed odd to Altara that there was no religious symbol at the apex of the steeple. It simply stretched upward and abruptly ended like an elongated pyramid.

"Time to do homework," Elena called across the hall to her brother. She heard a shuffling noise and decided Connor heard her and was working on his lessons.

Elena signed off from Dream Life II, finished her Geography lesson and decided to call Tanisha, her best friend from school. They talked about the spring dance. A boy in school, Tyler, seemed to like Elena. He was an exchange student from Nigeria. She hoped he would ask her to the dance, otherwise she would attend the dance with several friends from the Dance Club. Tanisha was as excited as ever and had already purchased a dress for the dance. Her boyfriend, Dwayne, had asked her to the event over a month ago.

She knocked on Connor's door about 10pm and said, "I'll be downstairs with mom if you need me."

Elena shared chamomile tea with her mother and made plans to shop for a dress for the dance on the weekend. She gave her mother a hug and went upstairs to bed. She tapped on Connor's door and said a sleepy "goodnight."

The next morning Anna made scrambled eggs for breakfast and called upstairs. Five minutes later she walked upstairs and tapped on Elena's door.

"I'll be right down in a minute," Elena responded, "Did you forget it's a half day today?"

"I sure did honey," Her mom answered. "Take your time the eggs will wait."

Elena threw on her robe, crossed the hall and knocked on her brother's door. She waited a few minutes then opened the door, "I hope you're decent because I'm coming in."

The curtains were still drawn but a little sunlight peaked

through from the sides of the blinds. Not wanting to startle Connor by turning on the lights, Elena called his name again. When there was no answer she snapped on the overhead light. Connor was not in his bed. She turned to look around the room, she thought he might have hidden in his closet ready to roll out and spook her but his wheel chair was near the window next to his bed.

Nearly frantic with worry, Elena threw open his bathroom door and moved the shower curtain aside with an awful worry that Connor had fallen in the shower. A cry of fear rose in Elena's throat. Conner was not in his room. She scrambled down the stairs and nearly ran into her mother who had heard her scream.

"Mom," she cried, "Connor's gone!"

"What?" Anna said, "If this is a joke it's not funny!"

Elena crumpled on the bottom stair, "Connor is gone his wheelchair is in his room but he's gone!"

Anna paled and ran up the stairs. Elena hadn't seen that look of horror on her mother's face since they heard the news about the accident. She scrambled up after her.

They tore through the upstairs, every room every closet and even lowered the attic steps to see if somehow Connor had pulled himself up there. Frantic to find him, they searched the first floor in case Connor had dragged himself to the lift and went down the stairs. He was not to be found. The basement revealed nothing either.

Both women threw on their coats and scoured the grounds, shouting Connor's name as they ran. After searching the common grounds they walked back to the house in tears to call 911.

"Please send someone quickly, my son has disappeared!" Anna informed the operator.

One hundred miles away from Connor's home Ginny Ballatore heard the report about the kidnapping on the nightly news. Tears filled her eyes as she listened to Connor's mother, Anna, as she pleaded with her son's abductor to release him unharmed. She explained to the kidnapper about his disability and need for daily medications.

Ginny turned off the television, wiped her tears with a tissue, walked into her office and turned on her PC to investigate the incident on police channels. She e-mailed Lt. Aiden Christianson, an old friend who lived near Connor's town of Robertsville, MO. Ginny and Aiden had attended conferences and forensic seminars together over the years.

After Jordan was killed, Aiden had been there to help her pick up the pieces of her broken life. She wrote an e-mail offering her services to the family of the missing boy: "call it a hunch or intuition but I feel that there is more going on here than a kidnapping."

Lt. Christian had returned with, "I always trust your hunches, Ginny. Connor's family has very little money. The father's life insurance and 401 K are dwindling because of Connor's medical bills. Anna is a part time English teacher at Robertsville Community College makes about 45 grand a year. According to her bank records there is no windfall that a kidnapper could count on for ransom money."

The next morning, after a sleepless night, Ginny got another e-mail from Aiden. He had contacted Anna and she had agreed to meet with Ginny. She looked down at Holmes who had laid his head on her lap and announced, "I can't very well go on an investigation without my faithful assistant can I? Don't worry Holmes you're coming too. This time I'm taking the Jeep."

It took Ginny about an hour to prepare for the trip. Her MS caused her to walk with stilted movements and sometimes only her cane kept her from toppling over. Her daily medications reduced the symptoms for which she was grateful. She had the kind of MS that was recurring and remitting. The wait for a remission was ongoing. The bottom line was, barring an unforeseen miracle, her disease was progressive.

Holmes, who loved road trips, was moving excitedly back and forth and in circles as she packed her overnight bag. He followed her into the kitchen where he eagerly accepted a dog treat. He was let outside to do his business and chase the squirrels one last time before they left.

Ginny packed a duffel bag of toys, blankets, dog food and

treats for Holmes which she put in the trunk of the Jeep on top of the Holmes' dog pillow. She attached him to his lead, let him in the jeep and they started off on their journey.

As they drove to the highway, she lowered the passenger window so the dog could hang his head out the window and sniff all the exciting smells in the air.

Ginny had e-mailed her two sons earlier to let them know she would be out of town for a while and texted them the address of the Jamestown Inn where she and Holmes would be staying. She had reserved a large suite with a king sized bed, sitting room and kitchenette. She was pleased to see that it overlooked the rolling verdant foothills of the Ozark Mountains.

Back in Robertsville, Anna and Elena sat at the kitchen table pouring over the newspapers and reviewing the latest efforts to find Connor. It seemed impossible to both of them that anyone could whisk Connor away without a trace. So far, no clues had been found. The only finger prints found were those of the family and Connor's friend from school, Drake, who had visited two weeks earlier to join him in an on-line video game tournament.

Anna's heart fell as she realized the search might be called off if some evidence or information wasn't discovered soon. The thought of her son lying helpless in an abandoned warehouse or trapped in a pervert's home nearly drove her mad. Feeling helpless was the worst of it. Only her daughter's presence kept her from losing any semblance of control. She looked over at Elena. She knew her daughter was miserable and blamed herself for Connor's disappearance.

Elena looked at her mother and repeated what she had said over and over again the last two days, "If only I had stayed on the web site with him. I should have told him to quit the game after he told me about that weird Preacher guy wanted to be his friend. Connor was so happy on that site." Tears welled up in her eyes, "He could be whomever he wanted and do whatever he wanted in a perfect body. Now he's gone and it's my fault! I had to go and talk to Tanisha about the dance."

Anna looked at her daughter and insisted, "It is not your fault,

Elena. Connor made his own decision and would have done the same thing even if you had stayed on the web site. I told him just the other day he couldn't drag himself from Dreamlife II even if his life depended on it. I am his parent and I should have shut it down weeks ago." She the touched Anna's sleeve, "So you see if anyone is to blame, it's me."

She walked around the table and put her arms around her daughter. They cried together as they had many times before in the last few days. Anna remembered that they had a two o'clock appointment with Ginny Ballatore. It gave her a chance to hope that she could help them find Connor.

Lieutenant Christianson had described Mrs. Ballatore as a gifted investigator with an uncanny ability to find missing persons no one else could find. He quickly assured Anna she was not a psychic and had no occult powers or strange beliefs. He explained that Ginny had a logical intelligent mind of a trained criminologist. She was good at solving puzzles some perpetrators concocted to remain elusive to capture.

Lt Christianson had described to Anna how Ginny had found a missing infant a year earlier. She had discovered that the husband of a childless woman had kidnapped the infant from her grandmother while she shopped at his toy store. The lieutenant explained how she had solved the murder of a beloved veterinarian in her home town of Olivette Missouri. Anna sighed. She wanted to trust this woman. She could be their last hope.

When Ginny B pulled into the parking lot of the Jamestown Inn it was nearly lunchtime. She checked in and carefully unpacked her clothes. Holmes padded around the room all excited about their new digs. He ran over to the window and stared out scanning the area for critters. Ginny petted him and opened the balcony doors.

She and Holmes enjoyed the breeze and warm sunshine. Because the Inn stood high on a bluff, a breathtaking view lay before them. Birds chirped, butterflies flitted back and forth, new to life in early spring, and dogwood trees blossomed in white and pink throughout the woods below. A silvery river flowed past the trees winding and snaking off to the right. Several fishermen stood in the water, cast their nets and tried their luck a few feet from a gravel beach. Clearly marked hiking trails dotted the hillside below and intersected at a wooden bridge that spanned the gracefully moving stream.

Pulling her gaze from the peaceful scene Ginny looked down at Holmes, "Come on baby, its lunchtime. Let's grab some food at the Jamestown Café. We have a lot of work to do in the next few days and we have to keep up our strength."

Holmes hopped up on two feet so his mistress could attach his lead. His tongue flopped out of his mouth at the mention of food. He hoped for a nibble of roast beef or chicken. If not, he knew she carried a bag of his treats in the purse she had retrieved on the way out the door.

Ginny's appointment with Anna and her daughter was at 2pm. She lived about five miles past the Junior College on the outskirts of Robertsville. In the meantime there was a good country lunch buffet to be sampled.

The inn had a decent diner decorated with early American wooden tables and chairs. A dark green tiled floor with American Heritage area rugs to warm things up. The many paned windows were dressed in red and white checked ruffled curtains. The ceiling boasted old fashioned lighting to look like tiny hurricane lamps. Under the counter enticing cakes, pies, cupcakes and cookies sat on the shelves of the glass display case.

Holmes was designated as her support dog and wore his official sign and tags on his harness. Ginny went up to the counter ordered lunch and the hostess led them to the outdoor dining area.

Ginny ate her grilled chicken sandwich and salad in silence and mulled over the case. Holmes enjoyed little bites of her meat and a cool drink of water from a paper bowl the waitress had kindly brought for him. Holmes looked up at his mistress and cocked his head. He knew she was deep in thought about the new case they were on.

The lady detective bowed her head and said a soft prayer. She was going to need the help of a higher power to solve this case.

There were no apparent clues unlike her other cases. Solving this mystery would require a lot of grace, if not an outright miracle, and time was running out.

Ginny B. pulled into the driveway of Anna Shephard's Tudor style home on Spring Garden Drive of Glendale Meadows Estates.

She looked over at Holmes, "Stay here Holmes. It's not time for you to meet the family yet."

Holmes made a disappointed little whine and looked up at her with questioning eyes. Ginny petted him and kissed the top of his head. He accepted that he would have to wait and watched his mistress as she walked to the door.

Ginny looked around as she made her way up the walk. She noted that there were no tree branches, trellises or vines that reached anywhere near Connor's room on the second floor that were accessible to an intruder.

Ginny rang the doorbell. The forest green door with its floral etched beveled glass windows opened to reveal a petite woman with honey colored hair. There was a haunted weary look about her. The woman's soft brown eyes were red and swollen from many tears and sleepless nights.

"Anna Shepherd?" Ginny asked. "I'm Ginny Ballatore. Lt. Christianson asked me to meet with you."

"Yes," Anna answered and opened the door. "The Lieutenant told me you were coming. Please come in."

Ginny followed Anna into a lovely dining room decorated in Early American style. Anna motioned for her to sit on a floral love seat, "Would you like a cup of tea?"

"Thank You," Ginny nodded, "tea would be nice but why don't we talk in the kitchen where you and Elena can be comfortable?"

Anna nodded in relief, "This way, Ms. Ballatore,"

Ginny settled into one of the cushioned kitchen chairs. She leaned her cane against the wall and said, "Call me Ginny, please."

The kitchen table faced a large bay window which overlooked a beautifully landscaped back yard. Colorful spring flowers decorated the gardens. Ginny's trained eyes did not miss any details. The yard was secured with a sturdy six foot chain-linked fence with locked gates on the side and at the back. There were no trees next to the back of the house. Magnolia trees, flowering dogwood trees and pear trees lined either side of the spacious yard. Beyond the fence was a length of common ground with wooded areas that abutted the neighboring homes on either side.

Elena, Anna's daughter joined Ginny at the kitchen table. Ginny smiled at the young woman as they were introduced. Elena was tall and slender with honey blonde hair like her mother's. She had a heart shaped face and hazel eyes. The girl had a refreshing natural beauty. Ginny remembered her high school days and what a judgmental crowd teenagers could be. Teen girls of today looked so grown up and acted so sophisticated. Some of those girls could be very immature and incredibly cruel if you didn't meet their expectations.

Anna looked up from her cup of tea at Ginny and commented, "Lt. Christianson said you were a private consultant and good finding missing children." Seeing Ginny's nod she asked, "If there are no clues just exactly how can you do that?"

Ginny put her cup down, "First of all I want to say that being a mother myself, my heart goes out to you and Elena. There is nothing more terrifying than having a child go missing." She looked from Anna to Elena and continued, "There were no clues found by the police but I assure you there are clues to be discovered." Ginny noted the questioning look in both the women's eyes and explained, "I know you are probably wondering if am some crackpot psychic who sees dead people but I'm an ordinary person with extraordinary intuition."

Ginny let her words sink in a few moments, turned to Elena and asked, "Elena you and your brother are very close aren't you?"

"We have been since the day he was born," Elena answered, "I was four years old and I already knew I had to help him and protect him."

Ginny nodded and rose from her chair, "I want you to show me Connor's room and the web site you two were on the night he disappeared."

Elena nodded and the trio walked up the stairs. Ginny noted

the lift chair and asked, "Was the lift like this the morning after you discovered Connor was gone?"

"Yes," Elena answered turning to her mother who nodded in agreement, "Connor uses it before we go upstairs. It's at the top of the stairs to use the next day."

"If Connor were to use the lift late at night would either of you be able to hear it?" Ginny asked.

Elena answered first, "I always leave my door open a crack in case he calls me for help in the middle of the night."

Ann nodded, "Me too. So does Connor, it's a house rule."

Ginny observed that the hall was covered with a cinnamon colored carpet with a very thin pile for Connor's safety. The first door to the right was Connor's room. Across the hall was Elena's. There was a bathroom between Elena's bedroom and her mother's master bedroom at the end of the hall. The walls were pale peach and various framed family photos were hung on either side.

Ginny gazed at Conner's school photo. He was a handsome young man with dark eyes and longish light brown hair. His face still had a boyish roundness and a slight smile turned up his mouth showing the dimples on his cheeks.

Anna noticed Ginny looking at the photo and commented, "That was taken two years ago before the accident. Connor doesn't want to be in photos anymore."

"It must be hard for your family," Ginny acknowledged, "losing your husband and Connor being injured like that. It's hard enough to be a teenage boy let alone one who needs a wheel chair to get around."

"It was devastating," Anna agreed tears in her eyes, "We were just getting used to all the changes and then this happens."

Ginny looked at Anna and then over at Elena, "I'm going to make it my mission to find your son." She gazed at Elena, "Let's have a look at Connor's room."

At the doorway she turned to Anna and asked, "Did you change anything in this room after you discovered Connor was missing?"

Anna thought a moment, "No, we left it just the way it is now.

We searched the house and the grounds and then called the police."

Elena nodded, tears welling up in her eyes, "I couldn't go in there again after I saw he was missing."

Ginny scanned Connor's room. His bed was unmade, his gray comforter was thrown aside and his pillow still had an impression of his head on it. Above his bed was a large movie poster of Tron, the movie about a group of gamers who entered the video game of the same name. Over his chest of drawers was a star map. On the top of the chest was a model of the planetary system. Books on astronomy were stacked on the right. A book of origami sat on the top of the chest along with 4 excellent origami sculptures; a bird in flight, a giraffe, a cat and a dog. Across the room there was a bedside table with a digital clock and a cell phone attached to a charger on the right side of Connor's bed.

His wheel chair was on the side of the bed a few feet from a large window with a view of the backyard and common grounds. Scanning the left side of the room, Ginny walked over to the door that led to Connor's bathroom.

She turned to look at the two women, "Does Connor always leave his chair on the right side of the bed near the window?"

Elena and Anna looked at each other. Elena thought a moment and answered, "Most of the time it's on the left side of the bed in case he has to use the bathroom at night."

Anna looked over at Ginny, "Sometimes he leaves it on the right side too when he wants to sit and look out at the stars. Last night there were meteor showers, Connor enjoys seeing them."

Ginny walked over to the window and lifted the frame. She gazed outside the window and saw that there was no sizable ledge jutting from the exterior of the home.

Across from Connor's bed was a smoky glass-topped desk which held his laptop and headphones. The P C was off and the only other thing on the desk was a notebook and several textbooks.

Ginny jotted down a few notes and turned to Elena. "Let's have a look at your room."

Elena's room was decorated in pale blue. It was much like

most teenage girls' rooms Ginny had seen. The bed, dresser and chest of drawers were antique white. Her bedcovers and curtains were a pale white with a tiny blue phlox print. Pictures of she with her friends were attached to the frame of the dresser's rounded mirror. An eight by ten blue framed photo of her and Connor hung on the wall next to the mirror. Posters of teen idols hung on her door and the wall next to her bed. Her desk was across from the bed and a pale blue laptop sat on it along with various textbooks and notebooks.

Ginny sat down on a boudoir chair Anna had pulled up for her and watched Elena as she logged onto Dreamlife II. When the girl activated her avatar, a chill ran down Ginny's spine. There was something menacing about the web site. It seemed to be a doorway into a fantasy world that appeared to be an interesting diversion that could easily become an obsession. A disabled young man like Connor could be an easy mark for any predator on the site.

The landscape and the avatars were very life-like but surreal in their diversity. There was a spaceport in the distance and to the right of that a castle with a moat. Ginny felt like there was more going on than her unfamiliarity with role playing web sites that made her feel uneasy. There was a strange feeling to Dreamlife II she had not sensed when she had viewed the other role-playing games her two sons had frequented.

As Altara, Elena's avatar left her elegant Victorian home she took flight and landed at her brother Connor's futuristic domicile. She used his password "Spock" to enter the two giant silver doors. His ultra-modern rooms seemed plastic and vacuous to Ginny. It was barren of any details that could reveal anything that was personal to Connor. Even in this anonymous cyber world he chose not to reveal any clues to his authentic self.

After the tour of Xavier's, Connor's avatar's spacious mansion, Altara added a vehicle into the game, a powder blue Thunderbird sports car. She raced down a winding road to the club she and Xavier had frequented, The Rave Palace.

At the club, other avatars were milling around amid the shiny table tops, garish lights, and loud band music. Couples danced in wild outfits such a super hero designs, black clad goths, and beautiful fairies. Many were sipping on tall glasses of colorful drinks and smoking cigarettes held in long retro cigarette holders. In a way it was like a cyber costume party, everyone wore an avatar, and no one knew the real identity of those they mingled with.

"I'll show you where I last saw Connor," Elena announced. Her avatar walked outside the club onto a white tiled balcony that overlooked the scenic countryside. Altara pointed to a white church building in the distance. The building was flanked by two enormous live oaks, whose lower branches drooped down over the building shading it from the brilliant light of the two suns overhead. The church steeple pierced into the sky as high as the trees but there was no religious marker of any kind mounted on its apex. Two massive red doors decorated with dragon carvings marked the church's entrance.

Altara got into her car which suddenly lifted from the ground. The Thunderbird leveled out and landed near the church. She exited the car and walked up to the building's massive doors. She knocked loudly, but no one answered. Only darkness and silence met her when she peered into the glass windows on either side of the doors.

Elena turned to Ginny and stated, "I went to the club and talked to Paul and a few other club friends the day after Connor disappeared but no one at The Rave Palace has seen Xavier since the night he disappeared."

"When Connor was taken his cell phone was still on the charger", Ginny stated, "There was no way for him to call for help. It's possible that he could have computer access from another source than his laptop. Hopefully his abductor will grant him access to a laptop in order to continue playing Dream Life II."

Elena looked over at her and said in a tearful voice, "I know Connor is in that church, at least I know his avatar is. The Preacher's got him! I should have followed him in there or at least tried to stop him."

Anna came over and put her arm around her daughter, "Even

if you had followed him that man would not have allowed you access."

Ginny leaned toward Elena and said in a gentle but firm voice, "Listen to your mother. Hear me, young lady. What happened to Connor is not your fault. He wanted to go with Preacher and nothing you could have said would have stopped him. It was his choice. It's time to stop blaming yourself. Your mom and I need you to be strong and brave right now because we need your help to find Connor."

Elena sniffed, and wiped her tears away, "I'll do whatever you ask. I want to help find my brother more than anything!"

Anna hugged her daughter and looked over at Ginny, "How are we going to find my son?"

"Right now we are going to make an extensive search of the house and grounds," Ginny replied, "Tomorrow we will create a new avatar to get Preacher to take notice. I know just the people to help us do that. We will draw Preacher back into the game and hopefully he will use Connor's avatar to lure ours into his trap. When we earn Preacher's trust, he will let his guard down and hopefully he will lead us to Connor."

"If he is not here, where could my son be?" Anna asked worriedly.

"We will tear this place apart," Ginny insisted, "and yes, Connor probably is not on the property. We will find clues as to where Preacher has taken him, but I believe an important key to finding Connor is in the game, Dreamlife II."

Ginny rose from the chair and said, "Let's start our search but first I will need something Connor has worn that has his scent, a sweaty shirt or dirty sock will do." She smiled at their bewildered looks, "Don't worry, I won't use black magic and conjure anything up. I brought my red bone coon hound, Holmes with me. He's in the car. His nose is our best tool to finding traces of Connor's scent and maybe how he was taken from your home."

Ginny went to her car to retrieve her dog. Holmes was itching to get out of the car, do his business and mark his new territory. More than anything he loved sniffing human smells and hunting for clues. His tail wagged a mile a minute as he stood alert and ready for action.

Anna and Elena showered him with hugs and pets as they led him into the house. Anna grabbed a dirty sweatshirt from the back of Connor's closet. Ginny put it under Holmes' nose and the search was on.

Holmes sniffed Connor's dirty sweatshirt. It was ripe and stinky just how he liked it. He sprinted up the front stairs sniffing the porch and the door. He streaked through the living room and kitchen, paused to take in the wonderful breakfast smells from earlier and got back to his task.

The coon hound paused and checked out the lift. There were smells from Connor's hands on the arm rests but they were old scents. He darted up the stairs and sniffed the entire hall.

Holmes turned around at the end of the hall and sniffed again he paused at Connor's doorway and looked at Ginny who was standing behind him.

"Go on Holmes, find Connor's scent," Ginny stated letting him sniff the sweatshirt again.

Holmes found scents in Connor's room. There were strong scents on his pillow and in his bathroom. Ginny opened the window and Holmes jumped up on the sill and sniffed. He let out a small yip.

Anna, who was standing in the hall asked, "Did he find something?"

"Connor's scent is very heavy on the window sill," Ginny informed her.

To Ginny's surprise Holmes leaned his head out of the window and sniffed the outside of the sill. The dog continued to sniff and let out little barks. Not only did he sense Connor but another male scent while muted was still present.

Ginny gave Holmes a hug, "Down, Holmes, let me have a look."

Holmes jumped down and looked up at her excitedly. Ginny rewarded him with a dog treat. She studied the window sill carefully and turned to look at Anna and her daughter, "Not only was Connor at this window but he must have touched the outside of the sill as well for Holmes to find his scent there." Ginny looked at Holmes who was still sniffing and reacting excitedly. She suspected Holmes had gleaned another scent in the same area.

"How can that be?" Anna asked, "If he leaned out that far, he could have fallen."

"Were there any unusual persons or vehicles in the area the days before Connor disappeared, such as delivery trucks or workmen?" Ginny asked.

"Let me see," Anna stated, "We didn't have any deliveries except the mail but that's not unusual."

Elena touched her mother's sleeve and said, "Remember mom, the tree guys." She looked over at Ginny excitedly, "They were trimming some of the trees next to the common grounds."

"That's right," Anna recalled, "They trim the ones closest to the power lines every year. They had one of those lift things attached to a trailer."

Ginny nodded, "They're called cherry pickers. They can extend up to 35 feet."

"How does that help?" Elena asked.

"I may be wrong," Ginny explained, "but someone could have parked and hidden the cherry picker in the woods, driven a van with a trailer hitch later that night, attached the trailer and used it to take Connor out of the window."

"Why didn't Connor yell for help?" Anna asked bewildered.

Ginny touched her arm, "It was Preacher, a man dressed like the avatar. Connor wanted to go with him."

Elena looked over at her mother, "Ginny's right mom. Preacher was Connor's friend. I don't know what he could have said to him but he thought it was safe to go with him."

Holmes continued his search of the interior of Connor's home. Holmes now knew Anna and Elena's scent too so he could tell if another person had been in the home recently. Holmes found Connor's scent in every room except the basement. He was unable to check the attic because he could not climb the ladder. Ginny checked it out thoroughly and found no evidence of an intruder.

"Let's check your back yard," Ginny stated. Anna led Ginny

and Holmes out the back door. Holmes sniffed Connor's shirt and sprinted out onto the grounds. He started at the patio detecting not only Connors scent on the table but the left over remnants of their last BBQ. He smelled nothing in the flower beds so off he went sniffing every blade of grass, bush and tree.

The back gate proved more interesting to Holmes as he sniffed around the gate hook and the top of the chain-linked fence near the gate. Ginny opened the gate and Holmes darted out to the common grounds.

"As far as I know, Connor hasn't gone to the common grounds yet this year," Anna commented.

Elena agreed, "We play badminton out here with the neighbors in the summer. Connor's arms are very strong and he can lob the birdie over the net from his wheel chair."

Holmes sniffed near the tree line and ran back to Ginny and barked to tell her to follow him. The three women followed Holmes into the woods. There was an animal trail and a partial clearing. Holmes sniffed excitedly near that area.

Ginny put her hand up, "Stay here and let me check the area."

Not only did Ginny find two prints made from work boots but further in the clearing there were distinct impressions of two vehicles.

Ginny waved the women over and pointed to the tracks in the dirt, "These are tire tracks. Judging from the distance between them more likely a van than a truck," she pointed several feet beyond the four tracks to a set of two, "these were made by the trailer."

Anna held on to her daughter, "You were right, Ginny. Someone drove a van into these woods hooked up to the trailer and used the cherry picker to kidnap Connor."

Ginny gave them a sympathetic look, "Your back gate is just wide enough for the van and trailer to get through but with the thick grass and the dryness of the ground those tracks are no longer visible."

"Let's check out the front yard," Ginny, "Just to rule out any other possible scenario."

They walked around to the front yard, Holmes in the lead. The dog found Connor's scents on the railing of side ramp, but they were faint. He sniffed the family car's door handle and trotted back to the trunk.

Anna opened the trunk and Holmes jumped up excitedly. Connor's book bag lay in the center, next to several recycle grocery bags that smelled delightfully of raw meat.

Holmes dipped his head and scurried around the circle driveway. Because Connor could not walk he found no footprints or scents of the boy on the lawn.

Not to be limited, Holmes loped to the check out the rest of the cul-de-sac. He sniffed the lawns, driveways, flower beds and strips of common ground between the neighboring houses.

Finding no clues, Holmes raced back to Ginny. He jumped up and she gave him two dog treats and a hug, saying, "Good dog!"

Ginny reattached Holmes' lead and the trio of women walked back to the house. The women sat at the kitchen table in silence. Anna, Connor's emotionally stricken mother and his guilt-ridden sister, Elena were teary eyed and despondent.

Anna rose from the table, "I better get dinner started."

"Can I order out for us?" Ginny offered.

"That's kind of you but our neighbors have been bringing food for us all week," Anna answered, "I'll heat up the pot roast dinner and we'll have some of the salad I made earlier."

Ginny gazed at the two women, "Please don't lose hope. We know now how Connor was abducted and that it was probably Preacher who took him. You two have been so brave and helpful."

Elena gave Ginny a weak smile as she and her mother set the table. Holmes aware of their sadness padded over from one to the other. He looked up at them with empathetic eyes. The two women petted him and thanked him for finding clues.

While dinner was getting heated up Ginny stated, "I'm going to enlist the aid of three special people to help design the avatar we will use to draw Preacher out into the open."

Anna and Elena gazed at her hopefully and she continued with, "My oldest son, Jordan, his fiancé Carlie and my youngest son, Matt and his partner, Tony. The avatar has to be believable and contemporary. My assistants are smart and well equipped to set this up. I'll contact them this evening. My sons are on Spring Break from college so they will be able to make it here by tomorrow. It's over a two hour drive for them so I will make a reservation for them at my hotel. We'll grab a late lunch and then meet you here about 3 pm."

Ginny looked over at the two women and reminded them, "We will find Connor's trail, even if it's a cyber trail. Have faith. Preacher is somewhere in this city." Turning to Elena she asked, "What is the name of Connor's cyber town?"

"It's called Danthura," Elena explained, "Everyone needs a secure password to enter the town."

"If Preacher has been successful luring young teens in Danthura, he will continue his predation in that cyber town," Ginny explained, "I am going to contact an expert in cyber security I know in the FBI and see if the other missing teens were logged onto Dreamlife before they disappeared."

"Do you think Preacher might take Connor to another state," Anna asked worriedly.

"In my experience, with predators like Preacher, as long as he is successful here he will not leave until he has added more teens to his collection. It is crucial that we create the perfect avatar to beat him at his own game."

Anna walked Ginny and Holmes to the front door. "Thank you so much for your help. You've given us hope. She looked down at Holmes and petted the top of his head, "You too Holmes. You certainly have lived up to your name!"

Back at the Jamestown Inn, Ginny logged onto her laptop. She e-mailed Jessica Portland, the FBI agent and head of cyber-crimes whose office was in Downtown St. Louis. While she waited for a response, she called Jordan Jr. and filled him in on the plan.

"Good news mom, "Jordan told her, "Carlie is in town too and is anxious to help with the case."

"Fantastic, "Ginny replied, "Carlie is the perfect person to create a female avatar."

"By the way, I talked to Matt," Jordan stated, referring to his younger brother. "He is packed and ready to go. His partner Tony is on vacation and wants to help out. We are driving down together."

"Wonderful news, I'll need all the help I can get," Ginny stated, Matt can create the buildings, and Tony is a whiz at music which will create the right ambiance for our scheme."

Ginny sat on the balcony with Holmes as the sun set. She opened her lap top and researched articles about Dreamlife II. She discovered that Connor was not alone in his obsession for that cyber world. Many disabled teens and adults joined the web site. According to a reporter who wrote for Cyber-World, joining the Dream Life II site gave the users freedom they did not have in the real world. They could be a perfect person that would not be made fun of or stick out in a crowd. Using their avatars, they could make friends they had things in common with. Dating was a popular thing to do on the site. Cyber relationships continued for months.

Holmes looked up at Ginny when she murmured, "That is so sad". He nudged her hand and she scratched him behind his soft furry ears.

Further into the article she gasped when she read a report from last October. The headline on the paper read, "Three Teens Who Made Suicide Pact- Found Dead!" It was a horrifying story about three outcast teens, a girl and two boys, all 16 years old. They decided if they killed themselves in the real world, their lives would continue in cyber world. She was in tears thinking how disturbing it was that the hatred and intolerance of others drove these teens to such desperate measures.

Ginny logged off and looked at the radiant sunset to the west with a heavy heart. Preacher was a cyber predator but there had to be more to the man than that. Why dress all in white? Why live in a church building?

Thinking about the Preacher avatar reminded Ginny of an old cartoon. In the anime, two strangers came to town, one dressed in black and one dressed in white. As the story proceeded the stranger in black turned out to be an angel and the one in white was the devil.

153

Ginny realized Preacher was an angel in white to the teens. He was telling them what they wanted to hear. He used their insecurities to lure them in the guise of a cool friend or mentor.

For Connor, he was a father figure to replace the one he lost. Preacher knew the boy's vulnerabilities. How many times have these types of predators become a second parent for the kids they abuse? In Ginny's experience it was an effective way to groom the kids for their nefarious needs. Ginny was convinced that she and her team could create an avatar that would flush Preacher out into the open. It was Preacher's turn to be the prey.

Ginny slept restlessly that night. A terrifying nightmare spoiled her rest. In the dream, Preacher had cornered Connor in the church. She was struggling to get the boy away from him. When Holmes attacked Preacher he had turned into a monster with horns and long claws. Her dog was lifted up and thrown aside like a useless rag doll. Cries of pain rose from the wounded canine. Ginny ran to Holmes but her legs wouldn't work. When Preacher zapped her with a bolt of lightning, she screamed and woke up.

She sat up in bed drenched in sweat. Holmes was staring at her in the darkness. He slurped her face and cuddled closer to her. After a few moments, a sense of calm came over her like a warm embrace from her deceased husband, Jordan.

In her mind she heard him say, "Hang in there babe. God will be with you every step of the way. I'll always be right here beside you in spirit, love. Have faith, grace asked for will not be denied."

The next morning, Ginny rose early to a beautiful sunny day. It was late April and the weather report stated it would be in the 70's. Inspired by the beauty of the grounds, Ginny put Holmes on his lead, grabbed her walking cane and headed out to one of the paved trails near the Inn. It was slow going but the fresh air and the sound of birds dissipated the residual effects of the previous night's restless sleep.

After getting a text from Jordan, Ginny walked outside to greet her family as they pulled into the parking lot at the Jamestown Inn. She gave them all a hug. She could tell her sons were glad to see that she looked well.

Their suites were next to Ginny's and Holmes danced around wanting to be petted while they unloaded their suitcases. Holmes was proud of himself as he carried in Carlie's smaller overnight bag. He got a dog treat for his effort.

As they stood on the balcony and admired the view, Ginny ordered a carry out grilled chicken lunch from the Jamestown Café. She and Tony set the table with the paper plates and Carlie made lemonade. Matt took Holmes for a walk to do his business, and threw his toy to him a few times laughing at how he would run like the wind to catch it then drop his head down and look up at Matt and give a little playful growl as if to say "My toy!"

The lunch arrived a few minutes later and they sat down at the kitchenette table. After saying grace and sipping his lemonade Jordan asked, "Mom, how can we help find Connor?"

Ginny put her fork down, took a sip of lemonade and answered with, "As you know the police, headed by Lt. Christianson, our dear friend, found no real clues. They searched the home and property thoroughly. There were no fingerprints left other than those accounted for. The grounds outside the property were searched within a three mile radius."

When she explained to him and the rest of the group her theory on how Connor was abducted, everyone at the table agreed that it could have been possible.

"What's the plan, mom?" Matt asked.

Ginny gazed around the table, "As I told you all in my texts, Connor was on the Dream Life II web site shortly before he was taken. Elena, Connor's sister, showed me the web site and I got to see how it worked. Everyone in the Peaceable Kingdom of Danthura has to create a password to participate. I think we need to use the web site to find him."

Carlie's eyebrows arched, "We sign up on the web site, create an avatar and do a cyber investigation?"

Ginny smiled at Carlie, "Jordan told me you design avatars for video gamers to use. I need you help to create the perfect one to infiltrate Dream Life II."

Carlie nodded and explained, "It helps pay my tuition at the

Art Institute in Kansas City. I have hundreds of designs on my web site but an original one would be better for this, some of the users may have purchased my other designs."

"I hope to lure Preacher back on the game with the avatar," Ginny explained, "Many of these types of predators want to find friends for their captives to keep them happy. Preacher successfully took Connor and I have a feeling he is not through with abducting kids in this area."

Jordan looked at his mom and offered, "This avatar who calls himself Preacher, could have a background of abuse too. I have studied many cases about them in my abnormal psychology courses. He is probably is an introvert and loner who finds freedom and self-esteem in being Preacher and having a lot of kids looking up to him."

Matt nodded and added, "Maybe he is a misfit too and was made fun of for some disability as a kid."

As Carlie helped clear the table she thought out loud to the group, "We need to create an avatar that is a compliment to Connor, a young girl around his age, innocent but a little sassy."

"Exactly," Ginny agreed, "A creative girl whose user is disabled and reclusive."

"I see what you meant," Carlie nodded, "We have to create a user with a background that attracts Preacher, whose avatar he would want for Connor."

That evening was spent at the table creating a user and avatar that would lure Preacher to the web site. Carlie would set up the visual profile, Jordan would create the psychological profile for the user and Matt and Tony would create the architecture and background music for the avatar's domicile.

While the trio was brainstorming, Ginny got a text from her FBI friend, Jessica Portland.

"Hello girlfriend!" it stated, "It was great to hear from you! I did that research on the connection between fantasy role playing web sites and kidnapping. I got a hit for Dream Life II. A young girl was kidnapped nearly three months ago and never found, Daquita Jones, from Atlanta Georgia. Keep me posted."

The group finished the draft profile and got together at the kitchen table to mull it over. The user of Dream Life II would be Liz Betts, a thirteen year old who had been the victim of a tragic fire, in which her twin sister had died. Liz survived but was afflicted with terrible scarring, in spite of numerous surgeries. She was home-schooled and rarely went out in public. Most of her free time was spent on web games and she joined Dream Life II to live out the fantasy life she craved but had lost forever.

Natasha would be Liz's avatar, a petite young girl with the face of a teen idol, high cheekbones, angel wing brows, large, violet eyes, full lips, perfect teeth and thick ebony tresses. Carlie gave her clothes a Goth look. The avatar wore a silver belted black tunic over shiny black leggings. Her feet were covered with chunky black military style boots. Her hair style was long with a shaved undercut. Some of the thick tendrils of hair on the top of her head were dyed blue and silver. The fingernails on her slender hand were painted half black and half dark purple.

Tony and Matt worked together to create Natasha's background. She would be an abstract artist whose works would be displayed and sold at her art gallery, "Rad Canvas," across from The Rave Palace.

Ginny had deposited $2,000 from her business account into Carlie's account on the internet for bit coins to purchase land and construct Natasha's art gallery.

Matt designed the white painted brick three story French Second Empire building. Tall beveled glass windows would adorn the sides and front of the building. The land and design cost 500 bit coins

Using the psychological profile they had developed about Preacher, Jordan created bright rebellious works of art that would reflect Natasha's troubled soul. One of the galleries main attractions on the inside would be a large portrait of Preacher, standing in front of the red-doors of the white church building.

Tony created a selection of moody clashing music to be the background for the opening of the Rad Gallery. He created a combination of classical, rap, jazz, heavy metal and rock tunes to entertain the party guests.

Carlie logged onto Dreamlife II, created a password, "Overtherainbow/dream" and the avatar was in place. The next step was to present the plan to Anna and Elena the following day.

Once their work was completed, Ginny stated, "You've all worked really hard today. I'm very proud of the results. Let's take a leisurely walk by the river and clear our heads."

Ginny put Holmes on his lead and they filed out of the Inn and walked to the Crowe's Nest Path. The day was breezy and sunny the dogwood trees sported their beautiful blooms as they traversed the path.

"You all go ahead," Ginny stated, "Enjoy the path. About a mile ahead, it veers to the right and leads back to the Jamestown Café. We'll have dinner there, my treat."

"Are you sure mom?" Jordan asked. "We could walk you back."

"Holmes and I will be fine," Ginny assured him. "I'm going to clear my mind and take my time,"

The quartet waved as they walked ahead on the path. Ginny couldn't help but think about the case. She knew it would not be easy smoking Preacher out, he was smart, clever and experienced at eluding capture. They had to peak his interest in a subtle not too obvious way so as not to drive him off the web.

"Trust," Ginny said aloud, causing Holmes to look back at her. She leaned down and petted him, "That's right Holmes, trust. Get Preacher to trust our avatar and he just might slip up and lead us to Connor."

The next morning the crew met at the Breakfast Nook in Robertsville on their way to meet with Anna and Elena. They talked about family and their studies and laughed at Holmes antics under the table. He was drooling and woofing for more scraps of bacon.

After greeting Ann and Elena, and introducing the team, Ginny let Homes out in the back yard to enjoy the day while the group filed up the stairs to Connor's room. She filled Anna and

Elena in on their plan, relieved to see the hopeful looks on their faces.

Elena knew Connor had taped all his passwords to the bottom of his key board. She logged onto Dreamlife II, scrolled to Danthura and opened the web world. She would use her avatar, Altara, to help the others become familiar with the site.

Carlie manipulated the Natasha avatar of her user, Liz Betts, as she left her third floor apartment and entered the first floor of her art gallery, "Rad Canvas."

Curios avatars walked by as Natasha placed art canvases and sculptures in the display windows. The display of unique sterling silver and amber jewelry seemed to interest many of the female avatars.

A neon purple sign announced Rad Gallery's Grand Opening the next evening. A large colorful poster told the onlookers that the gallery would have a tea and coffee bar during daytime hours and wine tasting on weekends. As Natasha placed the business hours sign on the door, Altara drove up in her powder blue Thunderbird.

Altara walked toward Natasha with a smile and noted that she was dressed in a silk tunic printed with Van Gogh's Starry Night painting. Large cobalt blue crystal drops hung from her pixie ears. Her violet eyes were luminous. Her velvety hair was spiked at the top with silver and bright blue streaks. Black velvet leggings covered her slender legs and she wore purple platform sandals on her feet.

"Hello, I'm Natasha, owner and resident artist," she stated in a melodious voice.

Altara who was dressed in a white peasant blouse hip hugger jeans and bejeweled sandals, smiled back at her saying, "Hi I'm Altara Star. This is totally awesome! Danthura is really short on creative art." She leaned to look into the display window and turned to Natasha, "There are a lot of empty walls in the houses in this neighborhood that could use some art works."

"I hope they like mine!" Natasha exclaimed. She snapped her fingers and added, "I recognize you! Your face is on the Marquee of The Rave Palace."

"I'm the pop star of the month," Altara explained, "guest singer of a very popular band, 'Crestfallen'. Paul the club's owner would love some of those retro psychedelic posters for his club."

"Thanks for stopping by," Natasha stated and added, "It's hard to be the new kid on the block. I know I'm young but that's why I wanted to join the town. I needed a place where I would be accepted for my work."

"Hmm," Altara said, "Age isn't a problem in this town, but how young are you?"

"Not that young," Natasha insisted, "I'm almost fifteen."

"Well, almost fifteen," Altara said with a smile, "I'll see you at the opening."

Two hours later after the investigative team enjoyed carryout pizza and watched Holmes do his very special tricks to earn treats. After dinner, the group went upstairs and logged onto Dreamlife II. Elena was on her computer and Carlie on her lap top.

Natasha took Altara on a pre-opening tour of Rad Canvas and offered her Jasmine tea. Altara commented on how much she loved the acrylic paintings especially the ones of the anime characters Natasha and other artists had created. She invited Natasha to join her at The Rave Palace.

The party was loud and exuberant when the two avatars arrived. Paul made a dramatic entrance landing in his supersonic ultra-light on the landing strip lighted patio. He wore a silver flight suit and everyone shouted and raised their arms when he took off his helmet and walked into the club.

Altara introduced Natasha to her club friends. There was Zander, who was best friends with Xavier, the emcee, Plato; the bouncer, Lokie; Marilyn, the beautiful blonde hostess; Elvis, who looked like the the Rock and Roll star and a Bob Marley look alike called Dreds, the bongo player.

An hour later colorful lights were illuminating the room highlighting the dancers. Other patrons were sitting at café tables drinking cokes and lattes. Brightly hued cocktails were served in tall fluted glasses. Since the users weren't really consuming alcohol it was perfectly legal. Smokers could stop outside on the terrace and imbibe in their favorite cigarettes, cigars and vapor flavors.

Natasha asked Paul about the designs on the walls of the club while covertly trying to discover clues about Connor's whereabouts. Altara mentioned that Xavier had been interested in the neon signs above the bar.

After Natasha stated she would like to see the old church on the hill, the setting of her latest portrait, many of the patrons mentioned that they had never been there. One, young man, Solomon who played the keyboard in the band, commented that Preacher lived there but no one had seen him in days.

Sol's friend 90MM offered, "We haven't seen Xavier either. Those two are pretty tight."

Altara explained, "90MM paid Xavier 500 bit coins to design a 1920's Gothic mansion and Botanical Gardens on his property.

"That's a lot of coin," Natasha commented with a whistle. "I certainly hope he turns up."

After they slipped away from the rave, Altara and Natasha took the Thunderbird and pulled onto Peaceful Drive to investigate the white church on the hill.

Altara stopped in front of the church and turned to Natasha, "Spreading the word about your new gallery and the portrait worked. Preacher just messaged me that he would love to see the gallery." Altara speedily typed a reply, "I let him know that his portrait would be presented at the Rad Canvas' grand opening tomorrow night."

Natasha responded in her soft little girl voice, "I think Preacher could be a mentor for me. I know he will appreciate my work. From what you and others told me, he doesn't discriminate because someone's young."

As they got out of the Thunderbird the web-site changed to Night Mode. A harvest moon illuminated the area and the live oaks and the church building cast elongated shadows over the front lawn and street.

Natasha smiled at Altara and said, "I can't wait to meet Preacher all the girls at the rave said he was fine and so mysterious."

"Xavier talks about him all the time," Altara commented, "I'd like to meet him too."

She walked up to the huge red doors and knocked. When there was no answer she called Preacher's name then Conner's. Altara tried opening the doors but a password window popped up and she didn't know it.

Elena then tried to use Connor's password to manipulate his avatar but it was blocked. "Preacher must have talked Connor into putting an avatar block on Xavier. It's a security system so no other user can steal your avatar and use it."

Back on Danthura, Altara announced, "Let's go see if Xavier is home. I miss him."

"Awesome! I want to meet him," Natasha agreed.

The two avatars got in the Thunderbird and raced to Xavier's silver mansion. Altara used his password, "SPOCK" to enter his home. Automatic lights turned on as the entered the large living room with a glass ceiling that displayed the Milky Way and a myriad of stars. The full moon was like a lighthouse beacon above them.

Altara called out and the only response she got was from a Pet Pal wearing the name "Rusty" on his collar. The cyber Jack Russell Terrier must have been activated when they came in the door. Rusty yipped and yapped and his little claws made tapping sounds on the black marble tiled floor.

Rusty quieted down and raced over to be petted when he saw Altara, who bent down and scratched him behind the ears.

Natasha exclaimed, "How adorable!"

The little Pet Pal scrambled over to her and rolled over on his back. Natasha bent down and tickled his tummy.

Altara laughed, "You made a friend. Rusty is usually very shy."

Elena and Carlie signed off of Dreamlife for the night and the group walked downstairs to go over the evening.

Ginny looked at her notes and smiled, "I think we've gotten Preacher's attention. We will meet here tomorrow evening and attend the opening of The Rad Canvas. Elena and Carlie you both did a great job on the website. Carlie, Natasha is believable and will be attractive to Preacher because her character is young and vulnerable."

"Thanks," Carlie said, "I tried to make her attractive but still an innocent young woman."

Ginny looked at Elena, "I'm so proud of you. You kept calm and did not push too hard to get to Xavier. You made it seem like it was not out of character for Xavier to go off with Preacher."

"I was scared the whole time," Elena admitted, "I was so worried I would put Preacher off and lose contact with him on the web site."

"Tony and Matt, you two did an outstanding job on the architecture and music. We are ready." Ginny turned to Elena and asked, "What is a good time for the Grand Opening to start tomorrow night?"

"Friday night users log on after 10pm," Elena informed her.

"We will all meet here a little before nine," Ginny stated. She rose from her chair and turned to Anna adding, "Try and get some rest. Hopefully we will have some substantial info to find Connor after tomorrow evening."

After a restless night Ginny and her family slept in until almost noon. Ginny had occupied herself with scanning her notes and more info about the Dream Life II web site until 2am.

The family decided to have a late lunch at the Jamestown Café. They loaded their plates at the buffet and settled down at a table on the patio. Ginny let Holmes off his lead after he had his snack and he sprinted off onto the grounds to do his business and mark his territory.

Elena and Anna spent the morning working in the garden outdoors, weeding and planting the bedding flowers that had been sitting in their pots for a week. After they finished, mother and daughter went back inside to clean up and get ready for Ginny and her team to arrive.

Elena, who had been checking her e-mails, ran downstairs to her mother in tears proclaiming, "Mom, I got mail from Connor."

Anna looked up at her, her hand going to her throat, "You did! What was the message?"

Elena brought up the message on her cell phone it read: "Hey sis, tell the old bird that I'm okay, Connor." Elena's phone buzzed again, this time it was a text, "Ginny and her family are here mom. I can't wait to show them the message!"

Anna went to the door just as Ginny and her team parked in the driveway. She walked out to meet them and said, "Elena got a message from Connor!"

Ginny put Holmes on his lead and smiled at Anna, "That is good news!"

They filed into the living room and Ginny let Holmes out into the back yard. The group walked up the stairs and Elena pulled up the message on her computer. Ginny looked at the message when it came up on the screen, hopeful that it would give them some clue as to where Connor was. She repeated the message out loud, "Hey sis, tell the old bird I'm okay."

Anna sighed with relief, "Thank God he's alive!"

Ginny looked over at her, "Old bird" that is an odd thing to call your mom."

Jordan offered, "I work with teenagers in a half-way house rehab facility on weekends and I've heard them call their moms that."

Elena looked over at him and stated, "Connor never calls mom that not to me and not to his friends."

Ginny brightened at that information and said, "It's possible that Connor just sent us a clue about where he is." She turned to Matt and said, "Matt find me a map of Glendale that gives us the sites to see in the city."

Matt clicked on google maps and searched for a Glendale tourist map. He sat next to his mom so she could look at the map with him.

"Let's check out Old Town Glendale. I heard it has a quaint shopping district," Ginny suggested.

Matt zoomed in on Old Town Glendale and he searched the legend below for places of interest. He located City Hall and the ancient water tower. He browsed various attractions and only found three places with the name of a bird in its title, "Grey Eagle

Distributors has an historic warehouse and distribution center on Portage Street."

Ginny shook her head, "Too well known. Hundreds of workers go in and out on their various shifts each day. Besides it leads right into the business district. Check something with easy access to the interstate."

Matt offered, "Mother Goose Daycare?"

"Not a good place to hide an older child," Ginny answered. "Matt look, what is that building near the old Route 66 exit that merges on the highway going west?"

Matt zoomed onto the location and answered, "Ye Olde White Owl Inn and Antique Shop, at 444 Frontage Street."

Ginny looked at the legend that Jordan brought up on his laptop, "This section of town is over one hundred years old. It's an historic district. According to the blue arrow, it's designated for rehab."

Jordan looked at his mother, "I can get an aerial view or zoom onto the street, mom."

"Just the street, please," Ginny said. She watched as Jordan zoomed onto the location bringing up Frontage Street.

A three story building came into focus. Matt looked at the architecture and offered, "That is a French Second Empire building, dormers on the third floor and probably access to a patio or greenhouse on the roof. It was a popular design at the turn of the century into the 1940's."

Jordan scrolled around the architectural design of the building, "Two apartments on the third floor, the main store front on the first floor, second floor living space probably for the owner and it looks like there is a spacious basement for storage."

Matt interjected, "Looking at the original specs, it used to house a stained glass window works in the basement." He pointed to the tall beveled stained glass windows on the second floor and the double glass doors at the entrance, "Those display doors for the shop were probably installed at a later time looks like 1950's style but blends in well with the older architecture. Matt scrolled to a back view of the building and added, "It looks like there is a stairway and access to the apartments at the rear of the building."

"Good work you two," Ginny stated, "Perfect location for a kidnapper. It's secluded enough. Preacher could come and go without being seen. There is a carriage house which obscures the view of the alley."

Anna stood up from her position on Elena's bed, "Should I make lunch for us?"

"Make lunch for yourself and Elena," Ginny answered. "The rest of us are going to have lunch at the Clark Candy Diner which happens to be across the street from Ye Olde White Owl Inn and Antique Shop." Seeing Anna's questioning look, Ginny explained, "I know you two are itching to come with us but Preacher probably knows you two by sight. He doesn't know us and we can pretend to be tourists while we check out the area."

"If you think that's best," Anna agreed.

"They're right, mom," Elena stated, "I have to be here in case Connor e-mails me again."

"Please let us know what's going on," Anna requested, "Elena and I need some hope that things are moving along in finding Connor."

Ginny touched Anna's sleeve, "We will keep you posted. In the meantime, don't give up." She turned back to Elena, "Keep thinking of things you can say and do to entice Preacher onto the web site."

As they left for the car, Holmes looked up at Ginny and woofed, as if to ask, "Are we going on an adventure?"

"Ginny petted the dog and said, "The games afoot Holmes!" She turned on the GPS and followed directions to Old Town Glendale. She had to smile at Holmes who was vying for attention from Carlie, Matt and Tony who sat in the seat in front of him. In between checking their notes they were happy to oblige the dog. When the movement of the car made him sleepy, Holmes finally curled up and took a nap on his dog bed.

The Clark Candy Diner had so few patrons parked out front Ginny asked, "Is it closed?"

Jordan used his camera to zoom in on the diner and answered, "It's open. I see a few people inside."

Matt offered, "Looks liked the area rehab has really hurt their business."

Ginny pulled into a parking space under a large Crabapple tree with bright magenta blooms and they got out of the car. The doorbell jingled as they entered the old building.

Matt looked at her and said, "Go ahead and find a table mom I want to take some shots of the architecture."

Beth, the waitress, looked at Holmes askance until she read his harness tag "Support Animal." She smiled and led them to a table that seated six by the window.

Matt returned just as Beth took their lunch order, and announced, "I can't wait to get photos of all the old buildings on this street. Turn of the century architecture combines Victorian and Gothic styles and is built to last."

Ginny nodded and looked over at Carlie adding, "I love the beautiful sterling silver and marcasite jewelry of the era don't you?"

"I love vintage jewelry too," Carlie agreed, "We should check out the antique shop after lunch."

"I'm looking for one of the sterling silver fluted pins that hold real flowers," Ginny added. "Lilly's of the Valley from my garden would be perfect."

Matt looked over at Tony, "I wonder if they have antique pistols I could add to my collection."

Tony laughed and commented, "You have exactly one pistol."

Jordan grinned at his brother and added, "Derringers were still popular in those days, weren't they?"

Holmes who had settled near the window looked up at the family and presented his best "See how hungry I am" look with his large brown eyes and huffed to get their attention. He was rewarded with chunks of roast beef and chicken.

After lunch they walked down the Clark Candy Diner side of the street. Matt took photos of the Antique shop building and zoomed in on the third floor dormer windows. As they passed the building he turned to take photos of the side and back of the building.

They continued down the street, not wanting to spend too much time at the Antique shop and arouse suspicion about their photo shoot. The group paused at a small oasis of trees at the end of the street. According to Matt's research it had been a vacant lot that was recently transformed into the picturesque Chouteau Park. There was a small Turkish designed gazebo in the middle of the park and a marble fountain decorated with large fish spewing water from their mouths. Turn of the Century wrought iron benches and faux gaslights completed its old-fashioned theme.

They paused at the dog park to let Holmes do his business while Jordan and Matt took pictures of the area. The group then crossed the concrete bridge and made their way up the other side of Frontage Street.

Ginny looked over at her youngest son, "Matt, will you put Holmes in the car and open a few windows? He will be like a bull in a china shop in that store."

"Sure, mom," Matt answered. He and Tony walked the dog back to the car. Tony put Holmes in the car while Matt took a few more photos of the area.

The shop was dimly lit, Ginny suspected it was to keep the fact hidden that a lot of the so called antiques were bought at garage sales all over the city. What was more disappointing is that the shop was disorganized. Most of the goods were rusty and dusty and not worth buying. Ginny and the others pretended to look interested so they could get a good look at the layout of the building.

Joe looked at an old ivory handled Bowie knife while Ginny and Carlie studied the locked Jewelry display cases. Inside a tall narrow hutch, Ginny spied a somewhat tarnished antique flower vase.

The wizened elderly proprietor of the shop appeared from the shadows, "Would madam like to look at any of the pieces?"

Ginny smiled and answered, "Yes, please the antique vase pin.

I love this brooch," she looked at the proprietor an inquired, "I noticed there are two apartments on the third floor. My son,

Matt and his partner are looking for an apartment in Old Town. Is there one available?"

The proprietor smiled and sighed, "There would have been about a week ago. A man and his son rented apartment C. last week."

Tony walked over to the group and stated, "What a shame, I'm an artist and Matt loves the architecture of the area."

While his mom and Tony talked to the old man, Matt walked down a short hall and entered a door marked "Employees Only."

The proprietor said, "I'm also the landlord. Your son and his partner could come back in three weeks. Apartment C was rented for only a month. Normally I make tenants sign a year's lease, but with the rehab going on I couldn't afford turn down the business. Hardly anyone comes to this end of town anymore. The detours make driving into Old Town a nuisance."

Ginny gave him a sympathetic look, "I understand. I hope the rehab will bring more business. I know it will attract tourists too." She smiled and added, "I'll take this lovely brooch."

Matt exited the private office and shut the door just as the Proprietor closed the old cash register drawer with a loud bang after his mother made her purchase. It had conveniently covered the sound of the creaky old door closing behind him.

Once outside the Matt raised his eyebrows and leaned toward his mother. He put his arm around her concealing his opened hand which held a key labeled, C.

Ginny looked up at her son, "Won't the landlord miss his key?"

"I don't think so," Matt replied, "They were in the small drawer underneath the hanging key holder marked extra keys."

On the way out of Old Town Glendale they decided to take the alley detour behind the shop into the business district. The speed limit was 15 mph and Matt was able to take photos of the back of the building and locate the stairs to the upper floor.

Back at Connor's home, his mom and sister listened eagerly as Ginny updated them on their progress. Anna put down her tea cup, looked at Ginny and asked, "You had the key why didn't you go in the apartment and get my son?"

Ginny gave her an empathetic look, "I know how you must feel. More than anything we wanted to get Connor out of there. This is a very delicate situation. If Preacher had been there, he was probably watching for any unusual activity on the street. We could have spooked him. He would have whisked Connor away and been a hundred times more careful. Because we didn't have a search warrant, we could have been arrested if Preacher called the police. What my son Matt did while commendable, was risky and illegal."

Anna looked down at her hands, "Sorry, I know you are doing all that you can."

Ginny shook her head and explained, "No need to apologize for being worried sick about your son. We must have clear proof that Connor is still there. We'll study the videos and photos to see if your son tried to make himself known."

"If you had been seen, Connor's life could have been in danger," Anna conceded.

Ginny smiled at her reassuringly, "Now you understand why we have to set a very careful trap for this sewer rat. Preacher has been successful at this before. No doubt he has stolen other children before and moved from state to state, city to city. We don't know his real name to get information on him but I would bet that he has no criminal record."

Elena looked over at Ginny, "What can we do?"

"We can hope that this success with Connor will make him complacent," Ginny answered, "he might let his guard down and be embolden to take the bait on Dream Life."

Jordan smiled at Elena and added, "To catch this particular rat we need a certain kind of bait. That will be the sweet and wild Natasha avatar."

"We have to get Natasha to form a friendship with Preacher and be drawn into his creepy scheme," Carlie commented.

"Mind you all it will be dangerous," Ginny said looking at each member of the team at the table, "We have to catch him in the act."

Matt looked over at his mother, "She's right. He probably has a sixth sense about protecting his worthless neck."

Tony took the kettle and refilled their cups with tea, adding,

"I've researched the psychology of the influence of music on the disturbed mind. I think I have put together the type of music that will intrigue Preacher at the Grand Opening."

"I will be the bait," Carlie commented. She glanced at Jordan who had a worried look on his face. "Preacher has to have a live person to kidnap. That is what this is all about, right?"

Jordan was ready to protest but his mom touched his arm stating, "She's right. Carlie made up the user of the avatar." Ginny looked over at Carlie, "You don't have to do this if you don't want to. I could call an undercover cop I know to help us."

Carlie took hold of Jordan's hand, "I want to do this. I will have all of you to back me up. I'm not afraid. The Grand Opening is tonight we don't have time to fill anyone else in."

Matt suddenly stood up and paced around the kitchen. He turned to the group. "I think I know what Preacher wants."

Ginny looked up at him, "Tell us what you think."

"I think he wants a collection," Matt suggested.

Jordan looked at his brother, "Yes we know that, a collection of kids to prey on."

Matt shook his head, sat down and explained, "I don't think he is that kind of predator. I think he is a collector. He moves from city to city joining the web sites, scoping out avatars and choosing his favorites to steal and keep for himself."

Anna gave Matt a puzzled look, "No offense, Matt but that sounds crazy."

Elena looked at her mother and responded with, "No it doesn't. Matt is right. Preacher joined the web site to find the best avatars, the most popular that are easily led."

"We have no proof yet that Mr. Smith, the name I gave to the man who rented apartment C for himself and his son, are Preacher and Connor," Ginny reminded them, "However Connor gave us a great clue with his text."

Jordan looked at his mother, "We have to find proof. We need to look at the photos and video right now before we go back there."

The team huddled together to look at the videos of the Ye Olde White Owl Antique Shop and Inn. Matt scanned through the videos he took as they were driving away through the alley behind the building. It was dark inside both apartments and a tree on the side of the property shaded the view. Suddenly Matt stopped the video and zoomed in on the tall window on the right side of apartment C.

Everyone at the table gasped at what they saw. A shadowy figure moved behind the curtains. Matt pressed forward and then froze the video. A person who looked very much like Connor appeared between the two curtains. You could clearly see he was propped up on his elbows and not standing up. A taller figure appeared behind Connor and pulled him away. The blinds were abruptly lowered and the boy was no longer in view.

Jordan hit the table with his fist startling all of them, "Connor was there the whole time!"

Matt moved the video to the side of the building. A dark gray van could be seen parked under a low hanging Locust tree.

"Looks like the perfect vehicle to use to kidnap Connor," Ginny stated, "Without his wheel chair he was helpless to go anywhere to get help."

"What's the plan? Matt asked.

Ginny looked at the group and explained, "Elena and Carlie will use the web site to lure Preacher in the open. Once we get Preacher to take the bait, he will set up a meeting with Natasha's user and attempt to kidnap her as a companion for Conner. Ginny looked over at Carlie, "You will be here at the Jamestown Inn," She glanced at Matt and Tony, "Matt, you and Tony will stay here and protect Carlie."

"What about Connor?" Elena asked.

"Preacher will probably leave Connor behind in the apartment," Ginny answered, "Jordan and I will be on the street watching as he leaves. Once he has driven away I'll send Jordan to get Connor."

Anna sighed and stated, "I hope Connor will be home safely later tonight." She looked at Ginny with tears in her eyes, "What can Elena and I do?"

Ginny gave her an encouraging smile, "I'll call you once we have Connor. I will also let Lt. Christianson know you need an officer here to protect you. Its' possible that Preacher will want to abduct Elena as added insurance that Connor will not try to escape."

An hour later, Carlie was with Elena ensconced in her room both on line manipulating their avatars on Dreamlife II. Altara, attired in a golden lame gown, got into her Thunderbird and raced to the Rad Gallery opening. Natasha greeted her at the door dressed in a dark blue velvet tunic and shiny black leggings. The army boots she usually wore were replaced with black suede platform shoes retro 1960's.

Huge golden hoops dangled from her ears and a chucky gold nugget choker. Her hair was streaked with dark blue highlights this time, slicked straight back off her forehead.

"Hi girlfriend," Altara exclaimed, "Ready to get this party rolling?"

Natasha nodded and handed her a glass of champagne, "I'm ready to rock!"

One of Tony's music selections designed to entice Preacher played loudly in the background as the guests arrived. "Black Hole Sun" was a retro song that gave a strong but haunting vibe to the gala was blasting from the sound system.

Many of Altara's friends arrived at the gallery and happily took the fluted champagne glasses she and Natasha handed them. They were ushered in to a spacious area. The high ceilinged walls were painted dark purple and filled with magical fantasy artwork. The floor was made of glass tiles and you could see through to the basement storage area that boasted more paintings, posters and sculptures of birds, giraffes, and other jungle animals.

Paul, the owner of The Rave Palace, attired in a silver jumpsuit, walked around the room and pointed to all his favorite paintings exclaiming, "I want that one and that one! There goes my bit coin savings!"

Ned, Paul's partner roared to a stop in front of the gallery on his sleek tricked out Harley, with Little Bo Peep the cocktail waitress on back. Ned put his arm around Paul and grabbed a glass of champagne. Bo Peep let her lamb down on its lead and screeched as she entered the room. She took a glass of champagne and headed for the jewelry case.

Zander, Xavier's best friend, walked in wearing the costume of a Roman Centurion. He bowed to Natasha and took a sip of the drink she offered him. He turned to Altara asking, "Have you seen Xavier?"

"I think he is still with Preacher," Altara answered, "He and Preacher should be here any time."

Natasha stated in a worried voice, "I hope he shows his portrait is the star attraction of my work. He inspired me." She pointed to a large covered canvas on a platform to the right.

Altara walked over with a jaunty looking gentleman sporting a caped tuxedo, a top hat, and cane, "This is Jecky, our newest member."

After being greeted with smiles and a glass of bubbly Jecky stated, "I'm the avatar of Dr. Jekyl, and Mr. Hyde."

When Natasha shook the hand Jecky offered, Altra explained. "Jecky is a mild manner Veterinarian during the day, but at night he transforms into a wild and crazy but harmless guy."

Jecky let out a maniacal laugh, "I'm not into killing ladies, I rather like them," He went on to explain, "I can't stand the sight of blood and besides there are rules, even on Danthura."

Sheriff Cody, dressed as Wyatt Earp in western duds, nodded to the group and shook Jecky's hand stating, "I can vouch for the law here. I have my six gun stunners and a sturdy cyber jail with an energy field to secure it."

As the time went by Natasha and Altara entertained the guests with a silent video display of famous artworks, movies and plays. Tony provided radical background music after the appetizers were consumed and dancing commenced.

The music stopped and Natasha walked to the platform where the enshrouded portrait of Preacher was displayed. The crowd walked over to witness the unveiling. There were many exclamations of approval from the guests. The likeness to Preacher standing in front of the white church building was uncanny. The live oaks on either side of the church looked so real one expected to hear their leaves rustle in the breeze.

Paul applauded Natasha and the other patrons followed suit. He bowed to her and said, "Bravo, Bravo! C'est Magnifique! How did you get such an accurate portrait of Preacher? I know you haven't met him yet."

Natasha smiled and explained, "Altara showed me his picture and described him so well. I just knew what to paint."

The crowd became hushed and it parted to let someone through, it was Preacher himself. He studied the portrait with a secretive smile and stated, "I agree with Paul. It is amazing! It's like looking into a mirror!" He clapped to Natasha and added, "Astounding talent in one so young."

Natasha looked up at the tall man who was dressed in white. She gazed boldly into his icy blue eyes that revealed no emotion and protested, "I'm not that young! I'll be fifteen next week. Besides, there are a lot of talented artists even younger than me. "She glanced over at Altara and added, "Look at Altara she's not much older than me but has the voice of a true diva already. From what she told me, her brother Xavier's only thirteen and is an awesome architect!"

"I humbly apologize," Preacher said, "Would you like to meet the talented Xavier?"

"Yes, that would be sweet," Natasha stated. "We have a lot in common. From what I heard he's funny and smart and serious about his art like I am. I've seen his photo, he's really fine."

Preacher laughed lightly, "He is as a fine young man. By the way, how much are you asking for my portrait?"

Natasha looked over at her art work and replied, "I can't sell it, not yet." At Preacher's crestfallen look she quickly explained, "I get very attached to my work. It takes me a while to bare parting with it. It's like I birthed this creation and I'm not ready to give it up for adoption right away."

"I understand completely," Preacher reassured her. I would never want to part with my hard earned collection either."

Altara gazed at preacher and asked, "Could Natasha and I see

175

your collection? It must be amazing, knowing how appreciative you are of the arts."

Preacher gazed at the two lovely young avatars, smiled and said, "It would be my pleasure to share my collection with both of you after the gala." He walked away then turned back, "By the way Xavier will be there. Don't worry about the time. I stay up late. My collection is better viewed in the still of the night, when all noise is put to sleep."

Elena put Altara on auto-mingle and looked over at Ginny and exclaimed, "I almost lost it when Preacher said Connor would be there!"

Ginny put her hand on the girl's shoulder and stated, "But you didn't! You and Carlie were amazingly cool. I'm proud of you and I know your mother is too."

Anna walked over to her daughter and gave her a hug, "I am so blessed to have you for a daughter."

Holmes who had stood up from his position next to Ginny's feet padded over to Elena and looked up at her with large brown eyes. Elena wiped a few tears away and petted him, saying, "Thank you Holmes you always know how to make me feel better."

Ginny looked at the group and stated, "We can exhale now. Preacher took the bait. He loves beautiful avatars and doesn't even realize that it gives us the power to manipulate him. He thinks he is in control and that's what we want."

Anna looked over at Ginny and stated, "I don't understand what Preacher wants. He acts like a pedophile but you said he is not that kind of person."

"Make no mistake, Anna," Ginny explained, "Preacher is a monster. He loves beautiful avatars. They are works of cyber art, flawless, beautiful ideals of perfect men and women. Not like their users at all. He sees them as frail, imperfect human specimens, unworthy of their avatars."

Anna nodded, "Why prey on people with disabilities then?"

Elena touched her mom's arm, "Mom, they can't get away!"

Anna gasped and stood up, "Not my son, not Connor!"

Ginny looked up at Anna and Elena. "I promise you both that Connor will be the one who gets away!"

When Elena sat back down at the computer desk, Ginny looked over at her and stated, "Elena, you'll be okay. Remember, this may be our last chance to speak to Connor. Preacher has fallen for our trap and is interested in luring Natasha to meet Xavier and join him. He probably wants Altara too. Be careful. Don't get over anxious and push Preacher. Let him go at his own pace. We want him to think his plan is working."

Elena re-animated Altara from auto-mingle and had her assist Natasha with the sale of stunning pieces at the jewelry display.

After a few minutes, Altara smiled and walked over to Paul and asked, "Paul, the gala is about to end and Preacher invited Natasha and I to see his private collection. Could you make excuses for me at the club?"

Paul's left brow arched, "I'm impressed! No one has seen Preacher's mysterious inner sanctum except Xavier, and we haven't seen him for days." He smiled at Altara and said, "I'll be glad to hold down the fort at the club and keep the crazies at bay."

He took a sip of champagne and walked closer to Natasha and whispered, "While you and Altara are visiting Preacher's lair, I will be checking out that amazing poster of the Bengal Tiger with a butterfly fairy riding on its back! It would look great on my office wall!"

Natasha clinked glasses with Paul took a sip and said, "Not a problem. If everything works out with Preacher, consider the Butterfly Queen my gift."

Paul grinned and announced, "Come on peeps, after party at the club!"

After the crowd of revelers grabbed their purchases and filed out of the gala and across the street to The Rave Palace, Altara and Natasha got into the vintage powder blue Thunderbird and raced up the hill to Preacher's domicile.

The web site had created a dark star filled night befitting a Van Gogh work of art. The full moon shone down on the white church illuminating the area.

When they walked up to the door and Altara knocked, this time the huge red doors slowly opened inward. What they saw inside took them by surprise.

The inner room belied the exterior façade's appearance in that the walls and ceiling of the huge gallery room were entirely painted black. Flaming bronze torches shaped like arm were mounted between each work of art.

Both women stared in amazement at the pieces on display. They quickly surmised the theme of the works. Natasha studied each work of art and turned to Altara, "I see what Preacher has done here. Look up there a Gorgoyle ready to take flight is perched on a ledge and right in front of us is a gigantic sculpture of a Minotaur with a look of grotesque hatred on its face."

"They're so life-like!" Altara exclaimed, "Look in that corner to the right a hydra is shooting out of the darkness. Its eight heads are each a unique work of art."

Natasha pointed to the wall behind the Minotaur, "That oil painting of the Gorgon looks so real. Her eyes follow you wherever you walk."

Altara nodded, "Creatures from a fantastical nightmare right in front of us."

Natasha agreed, "I think we just stepped into an incredible Greek Myth."

Suddenly, Preacher stepped from the shadows. The two women stepped back in surprise. If the two girls could have popped out of cyber space they would have but they had to stay the course.

Preacher glided more than walked towards them. His robes were shimmering bright white giving him an almost angelic appearance in contrast to the blackness of the room.

"Do you like my collection?" Preacher asked, not waiting for an answer he added, "I think I have achieved my goal. I've found the ugliest most cunning and vile avatars ever dreamed of. Delightfully hideous are they not?"

Natasha nodded and replied, "They are creative and fantastic works of art! Each one is a unique vision of the mythological creature they represent."

Preacher beamed with delight, "I call this room, "The Ugly." He waved his finger and a peach colored light on the ceiling above illuminated a shiny black satin couch in front of them. "Please have a seat, "he encouraged, "I have other surprises in store for you."

In front of the sofa a long black marble table appeared holding an ebony tray and a decanter filled with a cinnamon colored liquid and four crystal goblets etched with dragons.

"May I offer you a glass of wine from my vineyard?" Preacher asked as he filled the four glasses on the tray, "It's my cinnamon imbued white Merlot. I call it Dragon's Milk."

"I hope one of those glasses is for my brother,' Altara commented, "Xavier loves wine."

Preacher smiled, "Most assuredly it is, see he comes now."

A hidden door in the wall to the right slid open and a tall figure dressed in blue jeans and a royal blue dress shirt entered the room. Xavier took the wine glass Preacher offered to him and smiled, saying, "What's up sis? I have been closeted a few days. Sorry I didn't contact you sooner. Preacher keeps me working on plans for his properties." Xavier looked over at Natasha, "It's cool you brought Natasha. I really wanted to meet her."

Altara refrained from racing over to hug Xavier instead she said, "Hi Bro! Been busy myself, helping Natasha with her gallery opening." She turned to Natasha, "Natasha, meet my brother, Xavier Dartanion."

Natasha smiled at Xavier and said in an excited voice, "I've heard the skinny about you from Altara and all your friends at the club. Your designs are really futuristic and awesome!"

"Thanks, Preacher told me about your gallery. I've seen the videos of your work it's the kind of fantasy art I like." Xavier looked over at Preacher hopefully and added, "I hope I can see Rad Canvas soon."

Preacher offered with a slight smirk, "In due time. I wanted to get all of you together because you three are the most stunning avatars on this web site." He looked at the two women and smiled, "Which brings me to my next surprise. You two lovely young ladies have only seen part of my collection."

He walked over to the floor to the enormous painting of the Gorgon and pushed the eye on one of her writhing serpents. The picture frame moved from the wall opened toward them like a door. With a wave of his hand Preacher ushered the three avatars into the next room announcing, "This is the rest of my collection, 'The Beautiful'. I've collected the most beautiful avatars any web site could hold."

Altara and Natasha followed Xavier and Preacher into the next gallery. The walls were a shimmering white hue. The floors were finished with white marble tiles so shiny they looked like glass. There were no paintings on the walls and no direct lighting could be seen, the room just glowed with an iridescent light.

Life-sized avatars imprisoned in glass tubes were displayed in the room. The characters stood unmoving in their spots, like statues, with no evidence of cyber life. They were frozen in various positions and poses placed around a large crystal fountain in the center of the room. There was a lovely mermaid supported on an acrylic wave. Her shimmering red hair floated around her delicate face as if she were under water. Next to her was a white knight in silver armor riding on a Unicorn. His arm was raised and held a sword resembling "Excalibur," the sword of King Arthur. There were seven avatars in all, each locked on pause. At the fountain, silver droplets like fairy dust sprayed from the statues of fairies with delicate transparent wings.

Natasha and Altara, although horrified, acted as though they were impressed by the magnitude of Preacher's exhibit.

Altara looked over at Xavier and tried not to cry out. He looked frozen in place too. Preacher lifted him and placed him on the right side of the fountain next to a beautiful African Queen with ebony hair dressed in gold embroidered colorful robes. To Altara's horror a transparent tube lowered itself from the ceiling and covered her brother. His pose was serene but his eyes were glassy and dead and his face held no expression.

Preacher smiled and explained, "Xavier is now honored to be part of my collection, flawless and immortal to be adored and admired forever by those who will visit my gallery in Danthura."

He gazed at Natasha and said, "However, since no man is an island, even a work of art needs a companion. I hope to place you at his side." He waved a finger and the glass tube expanded to twice its size.

Altara looked at Preacher's maniacal grin and realized why her brother had been taken, Matt was right. Preacher wanted Xavier as his collection. In order to do that he had to eliminate his user, Connor. She grabbed Natasha's arm and as they moved away commented, "Well she will certainly consider your offer, Preacher, but right now our friends are waiting at the club for us. May we come back tomorrow and see Xavier?"

Preacher seemed to accept their decision to return the next day, "Of course Altara and you may join your brother someday too. After all you are family. I can expand the display tube to include three easily!"

Preacher smiled and led the two women to the red doors. He waved as they walked to the Thunderbird and drove away.

Altara tried to drive calmly away and Natasha smiled and waved happily out of her window. Once out of sight she raced to her Victorian Mansion. Elena ensconced the two avatars in a hidden room in her mansion that could only be opened with a special password. Preacher may have gotten Altara's regular password but Elena had created a cyber secure password only she knew.

Once off the web Elena walked over to her mother and collapsed in her arms in tears. She was still shaking when they walked down the stairs to the kitchen. Anna put on a pot of tea as the group sat around the table.

Jordan put his arms around Carlie who was nearly in tears and helped her into the chair. Everyone at the table was very disturbed about the session on Dream Life II.

Ginny took a sip of her tea and said, "Now we know that Matt was correct. Preacher is not just kidnapping children he is stealing their avatars for his creepy collection. He intends to open his gallery and charge a fee to visitors. He could earn a lot of bit coins that way."

Anna looked over at Ginny and frowned, "How can he keep the avatars if they already have users?"

Ginny looked down at her hands and said in a worried voice, "He can only keep the avatar if the original user gives it up."

"What does that mean?" Anna insisted.

Ginny cleared her throat and replied, "It could mean that he has to dispose of the user permanently."

Elena let out a small cry, "You mean Preacher might kill Connor?"

"We don't know that for sure," Ginny stated, "He has kidnapped Connor, but we know that he is still alive. We have to get back to that inn and get him before Preacher leaves with Connor."

Carlie put her teacup down and offered, "Preacher contacted me while we were talking." Everyone at the table held their breath as she explained, "He is coming here tomorrow evening at 7 pm. I told him I was here for a family reunion with my parents and that they will be out choosing the food at the caterers."

Jordan held her hand and said, "That's our opportunity. Mom, You and I will go get Connor while Carlie, Matt and Tony stay here to stop Preacher, just like we planned."

Ginny nodded, "We should all get a good night's sleep there is a lot to do tomorrow and Connor is counting on us."

The next morning the team rehashed their plans over breakfast at the kitchenette. Tony, who loved to cook, made scrambled eggs while they talked.

"Jordan and I will head into Glendale about 6pm and wait for Preacher to leave for his meeting with Carlie. Jordan will search the apartment while Holmes and I wait in the Jeep just in case Preacher comes back," She looked over at Jordan, "I'll text you if I see the van coming back."

Ginny turned to look at Elena and Carlie, "You two girls keep Preacher busy on the web site. Do whatever you can to assure Preacher you are eager for his approval. Keep moving about Danthura as if you are looking for Xavier as Preacher would expect."

She looked over at Carlie and said, "When I call you from Ye

Olde White Owl Inn take your place as planned. Matt and Tony will be hidden in the room. Once you see Preacher, I will contact Lt. Christianson. He will send a squad car to the Jamestown Inn to apprehend Preacher."

Matt looked at his mother, "Mom, what if our plan blows up in our faces and Connor is already gone?"

Ginny put down her coffee cup and stated, "Connor is smart. If he is not there he will leave us a clue. Remember his words, 'I'm closeted right now.'"

Jordan looked over at his mother, "Time to go, I'll get Holmes in the car."

The drive took 20 minutes but traffic was light and Ginny and Jordan arrived at the inn early. They parked the car up the street behind Chouteau Park.

Ginny waited in the car while Jordan put on his black hoodie and walked down the street. He walked leisurely past the Inn and ducked around to the back. He hid next to the shed and took out his cell phone and added a zoom lens attachment.

As he zoomed in to third floor apartment Jordan was able to see that the lamp was lit near the window. It barely illuminated the room. He spotted a tall silhouette that moved back and forth. The curtains parted and Jordan quickly hid in the shadows.

From his position he could see the back bumper of the van parked in the space near the alley. He zoomed back to the apartment but the lamp had been turned off and he saw nothing.

Back in the Jamestown suite, Matt stood at the window watching for any activity. He took out pistol from its leather case and loaded it, carefully putting on the safety. It was his mom's weapon, a gift from his dad to keep her safe for the times when he worked nights. His dad had taught them how to use a gun and they went target shooting together every month.

Carlie was at her laptop, busily manipulating her avatar Natasha at the club. She and Altara were to meet at the club. Natasha exited the Rad Gallery carrying a wrapped art work.

Altara got out of her Thunderbird and waved, "Need some help?"

"No I'm fine,' Natasha answered with a smile, "Just help me get across the street without a collision with some crazy vehicle zooming by!"

The girls walked across the street and Altara held the door for Natasha and they both entered the club. Paul's birthday bash was in full swing. He was travelling to Paris with his partner and would be out of town for a few days.

Paul saw the two girls and greeted them warmly with a hug. He grinned and clapped when Natasha handed him the wrapped painting. He ripped the package open and exclaimed, "Marvelous!" It was the Butterfly Fairy poster he had admired at the gallery opening.

"You have been such a good friend," Natasha commented," and you helped us with Xavier like you promised. I'm just paying it forward."

"Did you find Xavier at Preachers?" Paul asked.

"Yes, he is in good hands," Natasha informed him, then added, "Although Zander is a little miffed that Preacher is his new best friend now.

Paul laughed and stated, "We miss Connor too. He still has a few jobs to finish around town."

"He'll turn up soon, Paul," Altara reassured him, "He loves your club and he has at least three architectural creations to finish. The bit coin will bring him back."

Paul handed his new painting to Ned and they walked back to Paul's office to mount it on the wall.

At Ye Olde White Owl Inn, Jordan drank down a can of coke from his backpack. He pulled up his cell phone when he saw movement from the apartment. The stairs were nearly hidden by shadows of a low hanging Oak tree on the side. A figure in a black hooded jacket and black pants hurried down the stairs. He raced along the walk exited the wrought iron gate and got into the van. It had to be Preacher making a quick exit. It was too early for the meeting with Natasha's user.

Jordan walked around the shed flattening his body against the wall. He made it to the other side of the shed just in time to see Preacher race away. He texted his mom, "Preacher is on the move he is headed for the highway to west Glendale. I'm going in to get Connor."

Ginny came alert and texted him back, "Be careful, let me know what's going on."

Jordan texted back his affirmative, put his phone in his pocket and retrieved the apartment key his mom had given him after breakfast. He looked around before he walked toward the apartment stairs. He climbed them slowly trying to make as little noise as possible.

He used the key to open the apartment door and called out, "Connor, I'm Jordan. Your mom, Anna, asked me to come and get you. It's safe to come out now." He remembered Connor's words on the web site. He had stated he had been closeted for a while.

Only the dimmest light from between the curtains entered the room creating a long snakelike moonbeam on the carpet. He turned on the lamp and searched the apartment. The living room ended at a narrow doorway which led into a grimy kitchen. The small table was strewn with leftovers from breakfast and the sink was filled with dirty plates.

Jordan walked down a tiny hall, scaring a few roaches with his cell phone light. The bedroom door was ajar. He stood close to the wall and opened it so as not to expose himself to harm if Preacher had an accomplice waiting inside.

The queen-sized bed took up most of the space in the tiny bedroom. Over to the right of the bed was the closet. Jordan opened the door and cried out as something rushed by him into the room. A tan and white calico cat meowed and looked up at him with bright blue eyes. He bent down and petted the little feline and said, "I's okay kitty you're free now. I bet you don't belong in this apartment or you wouldn't have been locked in the closet."

Jordan saw a long string in the closet and turned on the light. No clothes hung on the hangers but he spotted a pair of old slippers on the floor. He noticed something under one of the shoes and carefully retrieved it. It was an origami dog. He immediately texted his mom and told her about the clue.

Ginny texted back, "Connor left us a clue. He was trying to tell us where Preacher took him."

Jordan brought up the map of Robertsville on his cell phone and scanned the points of interest. He texted back, "Gramercy Kennels is right off of 44. It has a photo of a dog on it." He checked the Kennels web page and replied, "I'm sending you the address now."

"Thanks," his mother replied adding, "You stay there just in case Preacher returns. Holmes and I will head to the kennel. Hopefully Preacher dropped Connor off there on his way to kidnap Lisa Betts."

Ginny merged onto the interstate and took the second exit to Grant Wood Avenue, the location of Gramercy Kennels. She drove until she saw the large business sign and pulled into the lot. There were no other cars in the parking area. She surmised that Preacher knew the business was vacant and decided to use it to hide Connor until he could abduct Lisa Betts.

She put Holmes on his lead, grabbed her cane and walked to the door. When she got there she saw a notice that read, "Closed for Renovations." There was a padlock and chain on the door which looked new. Undeterred, Ginny walked around to the side of the building to try the window off what looked like the reception area. She found a wooden packing crate, put it under the window and climbed up. When Holmes looked up at her with a whine she said, "I know boy, you smell Connor's scent here, don't you."

To her good fortune the window was unlocked. She pulled herself up and over the sill and climbed in using her cane for balance. She leaned out the window and looked at Holmes and commanded, "Stay!" Ginny saw a side exit door down the hall and opened it.

Holmes barked, paced back and forth dragging his leash until he saw Ginny at the opened door. He raced over and she stood aside to let him in.

Ginny let the dog off his lead and ordered, "Go find Connor!"

Holmes barked in response and took off down the main hall of the veterinary center. Ginny turned on the lights as she tried to catch up. Holmes barked again and she turned to the right. A ramp past two swinging doors led to the dog runs.

Holmes went to run number five and waited impatiently until Ginny caught up and opened the gate. He sprinted down the run until he got half way and barked to let her know he had found Connor.

Ginny petted Holmes saying, "Good dog!' she gave him a dog treat and searched the dog run for Connor. She located the boy at the very end of the dog run leaning against the wall. His useless legs were straight out in front of him. He gave her a wary look until Holmes ran up to him and licked his face.

Ginny smiled at Connor as he lost his fear and hugged Holmes, "I'm Ginny B, your mother hired me to find you and this is my assistant, Holmes."

"As in Sherlock Holmes?" Connor asked, "Cool!"

Ginny retrieved a cart from the supply area and said, "Put your arms around Holmes, he is also a trained support dog, he will pull you over to the cart."

Ginny looked at Holmes and ordered, "Help Connor. Bring him to me."

Connor put his arms around the dog and was gently dragged over to the cart. Ginny helped Connor slide onto the wooden base and she rolled it out of the dog run. Ginny took a water bottle from her back pack and gave it to Connor. He was thirsty and drank it all down.

She took out her phone and stated, "Would you like let your mom know you are okay?" Connor nodded happily as she keyed in the number.

"Mom" Connor said in slightly tearful voice, "I'm okay Ginny and Holmes rescued me."

Ginny could hear the cries of joy from Anna and Elena. She took the phone and let her know they would be home soon.

As they made their way to the side door, Connor said, "We can't leave Daquita behind."

"Daquita?" Ginny asked, Daquita Jones?" Ginny remembered

that she was the kidnapped girl from Atlanta her FBI friend had told her about.

"She was locked in here all alone for three months until I got here." Connor explained then added, "She is in storeroom inside the first room where they take care of the animals."

Ginny used a lock pick to get into the examining room. Seeing Connor's amazed look she commented, "I am a criminologist and I work with the police and because I know a crime has been committed I can use whatever means at my disposal to open this door."

"Awesome!" Connor exclaimed.

Ginny pushed the flat bed cart into the room and searched the desk drawer for the keys to the storeroom. She grabbed a key ring and was pleased when the key fit the lock.

A thin young girl was sitting on the floor of the storeroom holding a sack of dog food over her head.

Connor yelled to her, "It's okay Quita, she is a friend of my mom's."

Holmes rushed past Ginny and went into the storeroom. Daquita put her arms around the dog and hugged him.

Ginny took a good look at the young girl. Her hair was unkempt and her face dirty. She noticed the girl was missing part of her right leg below the knee. She handed the girl a bottle of water and turned away before Daquita could see her tears.

"Connor said someone would come for us," Daquita stated with a smile.

The girl put her arms around Ginny's neck and was lifted onto her one foot. She hopped over to the cart and Ginny gently lowered her down to sit next to Connor.

On their way to the car, Daquita told Ginny how she had met Preacher on Dreamlife II in a town called Atlantis. Her avatar, Mariah was a champion runner who danced with the bulls in the arena.

Preacher was the Oracle of the town and predicted she would win all the contest prizes. He wanted to meet the real her but she was afraid. He hacked onto her web site and found her address in Atlanta Georgia. He put chloroform on a rag, knocked her out and took her. The next thing she knew she was tied up and gagged in the back of his van and they were racing down the highway far away from her home.

Since she didn't have her crutches or prosthesis she was helpless. When tears filled her eyes, Connor put his hand on hers and they gripped on tightly. A shared trauma had created a lasting bond of friendship between them.

"Preacher let us be in the same room most of the day," Connor explained. "He brought us food and water and we got bathroom breaks using a rolling chair to get around. At night he locked me in the dog run and Quita in the office."

"How long were you at the apartment?" Ginny asked.

"Just that first night," Connor answered. "I made that origami dog and stuck it in the closet." He looked at Ginny and asked, "Is Patches okay?"

"The Calico?" Ginny nodded, "Yes, my son Jordan let her out and she ran to her home next door."

"She got in one day when Preacher opened the door and unloaded food in the kitchen," Connor said, "She kept me company and curled up with me that night. When Preacher took me away he put Patches in the closet."

Ginny looked at the two young teen and stated, "You two might be the bravest teenagers I've ever met." She opened the car door and Holmes jumped up into the passenger seat.

With some difficulty Ginny managed to help Connor into the back seat. His arms were strong and he was able to support his body and scoot his legs over. He leaned over and helped Daquita onto the seat next to him.

Ginny smiled into the rear view mirror and said, "Seatbelts please."

She passed back her cell phone to Daquita as they merged back on the interstate, "Call your family. They are probably worried sick."

Ginny drove down the highway and listened happily to the girl's reunion with her family. There were lots of tears on both ends. Holmes cuddled closer to Ginny when he saw a few tears roll down her cheeks.

They took the exit to downtown Glendale and drove to Ye Olde White Owl Inn. Jordan had gotten her text and was waiting in front of The Clark Candy Diner with two ice cream sundaes in his hands.

Back at the Jamestown Inn Carlie's avatar Natasha said goodbye to Paul and Happy Birthday as she and Altara left the The Rave Palace.

Before Carlie signed off as Natasha she waved to Altara, "See you tomorrow! Don't worry girlfriend, I just know Xavier will be home soon!"

Carlie closed her case notebook and hid it in the drawer. After she closed the window curtains to keep the room dark, she settled down on the bed and pretended to read. After a few moments she turned off the light, got up and hid behind the curtains.

Tony slipped into the suite via the balcony and settled in under the covers on the bed while Matt hid in the closet. He pulled the shuttered doors closed and waited.

After a few minutes Carlie heard a vehicle pull into the parking lot. She peaked out the window. The black van slowed and parked near the stairs to the second floor. That was her cue to move to the sliding balcony doors on the other side of the room and enter the safety of Ginny's suite next door.

Preacher, dressed all in white like his avatar, walked up the stairs and knocked lightly. Hearing no reply he entered the room. He walked around the sitting room looking and listening. He turned to the left and entered the dimly lit bedroom seemingly unnoticed. He crept over to the bed and gazed down at the sleeping form.

He removed a bottle and a cloth from his pocket. The smell of chloroform dispersed into the air as he wetted the cloth. As he bent over toward the sleeping form, the table lamp was turned on. The quilt was whipped aside and he gasped when he saw Tony, not his intended victim.

"Surprise!" Tony exclaimed.

Preacher backed away to make his escape and was attacked from behind by Matt who hit him on the head with the butt of a pistol. He fell on the bed and slid down to the floor, dropping the bottle of drugs. He moaned loudly and touched the gash on his head that dripped blood.

A plain clothes police officers who had been parked around the side of the building and alerted by Matt, burst into the room. She saw the perpetrator was down and pulled his hands behind his back and cuffed him.

Officer Tracy Brown called for backup and a second officer came into the suite to escort Preacher to the squad car. Tracy looked over at Matt and Tony and smiled, "Looks like you two had this under control." When the two men grinned back at her she added, "Thanks for making my job easier." She jotted down her report and waved goodbye.

Carlie and Matt walked outside as Preacher was placed in the back of the police cruiser. The kidnapper was grimacing from pain and his face was contorted in anger and frustration. He yelled at them in a high screeching voice, "They're mine! The avatars are mine!"

Ginny pulled up as the cruiser pulled away. She gazed over at Preacher and he stared back at her. Holmes leaned out the window and barked at the man whose smell he hated. Preacher, startled by the dog, cowered back on the seat of the cruiser.

"The tables are turned now, Preacher," Ginny stated, "You will be part of a collection of a rough group of convicts. I hope you know that they don't take kindly to men who abuse kids."

Later that evening Ginny, her family and Connor's family celebrated his return with a carryout pizza dinner.

Anna had hugged Daquita warmly and given her a pair of crutches to use. Elena took her up to her room and gave her a clean set of clothes. She helped her brush her hair to look nice when her parents arrived. They had been overjoyed and had never given up hope that they would get their beautiful daughter back. Soon her parents would be on a plane to Missouri. In a few hours they would land at Lambert International Airport where they would rent a car and be reunited with Daquita before morning.

Ginny put her pizza down and looked at the two rescued teens and smiled. She had a feeling they would remain close friends.

She gazed at Connor and asked, "Connor, do you think you'll go back on Dream Life II in the near future?"

The boy looked over at his mom and sister and shook his head, "Not a chance!" He grinned at Daquita and added, "I guess it's not so bad being me after all."

Printed in the United States
by Baker & Taylor Publisher Services